The Reckoning

Jack Compton

1

I can't wait any longer. I need answers.

A quick check in the mirror; black sweatpants, hoodie, snood and dark gloves. The only piece of me visible is a thin line above and around my eyes.

I listen for the faintest sound. Nothing. Except for the sounds of a house on a cold night.

A deep breath and then I'm down the stairs, treading on the parts closest to the wall to minimise creaking. Then through the kitchen, out of the back door and down the side of house to the front wall.

My breath forms a cloud of steam as I stand still to check. There's no movement in the suburban street, just a static view of pedestrian paths and lawned gardens, edged with hedges and fences. Frost has already formed on the cars parked on driveways.

Now.

I run to the corner wall of the target house and stop, listening hard over the pounding of my heart. No sounds.

Dropping my head down, I slip round to the back of the house, straining my eyes. Only one room with a light on. I know he'll be there but that's not enough. I need proof.

I pull out my phone, dim the screen and switch the camera on.

2

Above me, part-drawn curtains block the view. I have to stretch my arm to find a view through the gap.

The room is obviously a study, shelves unevenly lined with books and journals and a large monitor set up on a desk The lighting shifts and I yank the phone down; fear of discovery overriding simple common sense that says sudden movement is most likely to draw his attention.

Fuck.

I shrink back, watching the shadows on the ground change. A looming darkness forms and then the curtains are drawn sharply back, flooding the area in front of me with light. I hear the lock on the window twist and I scramble out of sight, hiding around the side of the house. The window is flung open and the man inside calls out; a calm, gentle manipulation:

"Are you alright?"

As if he cares. Nice try but you'd need to be dumb to fall for it. I stay silent and still, waiting for long seconds until there's a click and the window is locked.

I slump down to the ground. I want to leave but I can't. I haven't got what I need yet.

A minute passes as I give the man time to settle and then gingerly, I slide back to the study window. The curtains are now drawn, but there is a small line of light between them. That's enough to film.

Clicking to start video mode, I hold the phone up above my head and point the camera lens, looking up to see what is being recorded.

He's in there. His back is towards me and he's facing a computer monitor, a phone held up to his ear. He's animated but I can't hear the conversation. He shakes his head then drops the phone angrily, getting up from his chair, walking away from the computer. The light in the study goes off, leaving only blue light from the monitor illuminating the room.

I turn the camera towards the monitor, zooming in on the shadowy figure depicted on the screen. There's something in the figure's hand.

A gut-wrenching dread washes over me.

That figure is me.

3

I look up above me and my gut tightens. There's an infra-red camera.

Shit.

This time I don't hesitate. The phone goes inside my hoodie and I'm off, sprinting to the far side of the house, across the back stretch of lawn and diving behind the dark shape of a large, evergreen bush.

I curl up into a ball, turning my head in. I cannot be seen now. A few deep breaths and then my breathing becomes more controlled, as I wait to hear the sound of someone searching. Minutes pass but there's nothing to hear except the far-off noise of traffic and a distant siren. Slowly I turn my head and look back towards the house. All the lights are off now and it looks for all the world as if the occupant has gone to bed. I somehow doubt it but there is definitely no sign of him in the back garden.

I need to get out of here quickly. Cautiously, I crawl out of the bush and stand still as I look at the six-foot fence on this side of the house. I can do this. I run towards the corner of the fence, where it is attached to the wall and plant my foot three feet up on the wall and push off hard, momentum and the power of the thrust shoving me up as my hands catch the top of the fence, my torso twists and the rest of my body crashes over the fence and down to the ground on the other side. Picking myself up, I sprint across the front lawn and back onto the street. For a split-second I look behind me, seeing no sign of anyone following, the empty street broken only by a black car parked by a driveway.

I turn back to face home and begin to run, sprinting towards safety, even as my mind is processing what I've just seen.

And I realise the scale of the mistake I've made.

4

It's the car.

It's all wrong.

It wasn't there earlier.

There is no frost on the vehicle and there's a man sitting in the driver's seat. And I'm on the road.

I twist round to check it out and dazzling headlights come on, blinding me. I can't see but I know it's heading straight towards me, accelerating hard, the power of its four electric motors driving it faster and faster. With a dreadful insight, I realise there's no time to get out of the way.

The car hits me with terrifying force and I feel myself lifted high up in the air, the scream torn from my lips as my shoulders bang ferociously against the windscreen and my head catches the edge of the roofline. I can't feel my bent and broken legs hanging uselessly beneath me and I won't feel the rest of the somersault or the bone shattering thud as I come back down to earth. And I don't hear the sickening groan as the air is expelled from my body.

The car picks up pace and squeals away from my broken body.

5

In the house next door, the film ended a couple of hours ago, but she is still lying there; her mouth hanging open, a line of dribble dangling from the corner of her mouth, leaving a damp patch on her top.

Then Janet's eyes open. Something has cut into her peaceful sofa doze and brought her round. She isn't moving yet; her mind is still trying to work out what has just happened. She thinks she heard a scream. Not a TV scream but a real scream that, even in her confused state, burned through her mind, stirring a primeval instinct that hears both raw pain and rampant fear and wakes her in response.

Anxiously she shucks off the cerise pink throw that her husband had placed over her when he went to bed and heads for the window. She leans on the window ledge and rubs her eyes, scanning the scene outside for the source of the scream. There is nothing to be seen. Nothing but a lump of black on the roadway. It looks as though a fox has dragged a bin bag across the road before being disturbed. She is about to turn when she sees the front door of a house opposite open. A man is running towards the shape in the road. Then she looks again at the bin bag and realises she has got it all wrong.

It's a person.

She rushes to her own front door, pulls on a pair of wellington boots, slides her arms into a puffer jacket and swings open the door. In the roadway the man is bent over the person. His face turns towards her and she recognises the overweight figure of one of her neighbours. Even though he isn't wearing his trademark jacket with pocket square flowering out over the top pocket, she knows it's him. She sees the salt and pepper beard and hears his throaty voice. It's the doctor.

"Quickly," he calls out to her. "Can you phone for an ambulance immediately? There's been some kind of a dreadful accident."

She stops still, torn between the desire to get closer and see who has been hurt and wanting to be helpful. But the tone of the doctor's instruction tells her that the person on the ground must be really badly hurt and she decides to follow his instruction. Whoever it is out there, she thinks, they are lucky that the first person to get to her happens to be a doctor.

She doesn't know the truth.

6

Janet pats her pockets frantically and then shouts out:

"I haven't got my phone Doctor."

He wants her gone. Not for long. Just long enough.

"Well go and get the damn thing. NOW!"

She doesn't argue. She hurries back to her home, her boots flopping noisily as she half-jogs back indoors.

Behind her the doctor shifts the grip of his hands, slipping a hand on to each side of the victim's face and holding it tightly as he snarls at the critically injured girl.

"So you thought it was a good idea, did you? You were warned. It couldn't have been clearer. But still you wanted to know more. Did you not understand how big this is? Did you think it wouldn't matter?"

The doctor turns his head, looking around to check that no-one else is near. Satisfied, he returns to the girl, tightening his grip on her cheekbones. He lifts her head right up and then slams it hard back on the asphalt, wincing slightly as the sound of her skull mashing into the asphalt reaches his ears.

7

He can hear footsteps, so he begins talking softly:

"Shhh, shhh. Help is on its way."

Behind him a voice calls out:

"Doctor? Doctor?"

Janet is rushing back now, waving the phone in her hand.

"Do you want to talk to the ambulance people?" she asks as she gets closer. She places the phone into his outstretched hand.

She wants to ask how the girl is but the man's body language tells her the answer even before he speaks.

"Hello? Yes, it's Dr Samza here. It's too late, I'm afraid. She's gone. Can you tell the Police it looks like it's a FATACC? Yes, I am a police doctor on call. Have you already got the address?"

Janet looks down at the girl. She recognises the broken body as Chloe Robinson.

"What a tragic waste," she says absently.

Samza gives her back her phone.

"I'm sorry," he says, "there was nothing I could do. It was just too late. All we can do is wait for the police I'm afraid. Do you have a blanket we can cover the girl with?"

Moments later, the girl's body has been covered in cerise pink and Samza is telling her not to worry her as she apologises repeatedly for the state of the throw. He encourages her to leave and make a cup of sweet tea, putting his arm around her shoulders, turning her around and pointing her back home. A gentle push and she's gone.

Blue lights flicker on the trees as an ambulance appears and the doctor waves frantically causing the vehicle to draw to a halt a few yards away.

The doors open and the emergency technicians jump out and hurry over.

"What happened?" asks the taller of the two.

8

Dr Samza is explaining what happened:

"I heard a scream and when I got here, she was gone. Just too far gone."

The technician pulls the cover down off the girl's face. Even though he's experienced, he still winces at the sight in front of him.

"She really got whacked," he sighs.

"I'll say," agrees the doctor, struggling to hold off a smile, a smile that disappears a second later as the kneeling paramedic calls out sharply, his hand waving at his colleague.

"Hey! She's trying to breathe. Give me the bag quickly."

"Are you sure?" asks the doctor. "It's probably just that you've moved her, isn't it? Let me have a look. "

The doctor reaches down once more and puts his ear to the girl's mouth, listening for any sounds, checking for any flow of air.

"I can't hear anything. Can't feel a sinus rhythm either. But let's try anyway."

Kneeling up now, he begins CPR while one paramedic checks for breath before setting up an ambu-bag and the other connects a defibrillator and tries an initial charge. The machine shows a ventricular fibrillation and so they charge once more. This time there is a sinus rhythm and the atmosphere changes as they work fast to get the girl on a board, onto the gurney and onto the ambulance.

"I'll come with you," volunteers the doctor. "I know you'll need an extra set of hands to keep her alive," he adds, jumping into the vehicle and watching as the paramedic gets an oxygen mask on the girl's face and rearranges the defibrillator leads.

"I'll fix a cannula," says Samza.

Less than a minute later, the driver shouts that he's ready to go and the vehicle begins to move off, swinging round in a wide U-turn and then building up speed.

As the vehicle rocks around, Samza clumsily drops the cannula he is about to place in the girl's arm, swears loudly and shouts to the paramedic to grab him another. As soon as the man's back is turned, the doctor jabs the girl's throat hard with the edge of his hand. Immediately an alarm sounds.

"She's struggling to breathe," he says, "and I think she's going to arrest again."

He steps back and lets the paramedic reach across, check the monitor, seeing the heart rate slow. Moments later the girl's heart gives up and despite several more attempts to shock her back to life, there is no response.

Even though they are only two minutes away from the hospital, Samza reaches over to rest his hand on the paramedic's shoulder and tells him to stop.

"Don't take it hard. She was already gone at the scene," he says. "This was just a last-minute near-miracle. I've seen it before, you know. Patients holding on for one last, and often futile, attempt.

The technician rolls his eyes at the loss of a life.

"I'll never stop hating when they don't make it," he says.

"The day you do is the day the day to quit," says the doctor.

9

The damaged black Tesla is now 4 miles away from the scene of the crime. Inside, 'Roman' Phil is smiling. Most of his jobs require some real skill and driving ability. This one was one of the easiest. A simple wait and accelerate. There hadn't been a need to reverse. Not with the kind of force he had hit her with. All credit to the technology boffins, he supposes. The power of this beast is quite incredible and, apart from the slightest whine and the tyre noise, it is a silent and stunningly powerful weapon. The repair work might take a while, but he can wait until the heat is off before getting it sorted. At least he's £5000 richer than at the start of the night.

Now all he needs to do is pilot it safely back. At this time of night there shouldn't be any traffic and he'll be home with a beer in hand in less than 30 minutes.

If all goes well that is.

And it won't.

Police Traffic Officer Jim Spelden, known as Pitbull, both for his tenacity in a car chase and his stature, is parked up on the grass verge by the side of the dual carriageway, chewing thirty-six times on each mouthful of a tuna sandwich. He's trying to lose some weight and he remembers reading somewhere that chewing a lot helps to make you feel full up. It hadn't worked when he'd had his last meal break though, so he'd taken remedial measures by way of a quick stop at the petrol station where he'd picked up another sandwich to try again. Whether it worked or not, this should be enough to see him through the rest of the night shift. This time he decides to give up on the technique and reverts to his more usual speed of eating. A wise and sensible decision, he tells himself because, in the distance, he can see a dark-coloured car rapidly approaching him and it only has one headlight working.

He fills his mouth with the remainder of the sandwich and once the vehicle reaches him, he pulls out behind it, noting as it drives by that the windscreen of the vehicle is broken too and there are no number plates visible. Accelerating hard, it only takes him a minute to catch up with the car.

Roman Phil has seen the car pull out and come up quickly behind him. He'd seen that it is a silver BMW 5 series, which means it will almost certainly be an unmarked police car. Could be a drunk businessman who'd stopped for a piss by the side of the road though, but it pays to be careful at this point.

So Phil slows a little, allowing the BMW to pass if it wants to, yet the car stays doggedly behind him. He drops his speed a little more, now doing barely fifty-five on the dual carriageway. It's still behind him. Which means it must be a police car.

Fuck. He's going to have to try and get away.

The risks have just gone up.

10

He needs to get away. And that takes the right timing. He knows the police car will follow him for a while. They'll check out the number plate. Which won't be a problem. A cloned plate will buy him a little time.

Another glance in the mirror and he squeezes the accelerator, taking the car up to eighty miles an hour, driving past the junction he had originally planned to take. The BMW follows, and Phil's eyes contract sharply as his mirror reflects flashing headlights and the inevitable strobing blue lights.

Gunning the accelerator, he takes off fast, watching the speedometer increase until it reaches 140 mph a few seconds later. The police car is falling well back now and Phil smiles, certain that he can get off the road quickly and then he will be able to lose the BMW easily. He rounds the next bend and slams the brakes on hard, feeling the back end of the car lighten up as the weight of momentum transfers to the front tyres and, with a flick of his hand, he twists the wheel, expertly allowing the back end to break out and help turn the car as he mashes the accelerator down and hears the wheels slide and spin before they grip hard and launch him down the side road.

A twist of his fingers turns the car lights off and the night vision camera on. It's not perfect but he can clearly see the edges of the road as he slaloms away. In the mirror he can see the blue lights flickering but still following some way behind. His car is at the limits of adhesion as he slides around a bend, the four-wheel drive keeping him on the track until he reaches a large farm gate on his left. He presses down hard on the brakes just as he gets there, slides through the gate and comes to a sharp stop and puts the car into Park.

11

Pitbull glances at the lights ahead of him. He's working hard to catch up but he doesn't know the road well and doesn't want to end up in a ditch. He's on the radio to give a location and request assistance as the Tesla disappears around a distant bend. He is still waiting for a response as he winds his car through the bend and sees only darkness.

Fuck.

His own lights pick out a turning ahead but he can't brake in time. He reverses, switches gears and swings into the lane, scanning the landscape ahead, picking out farm buildings in the distance. Pitbull smiles: the idiot driver probably thinks the lights going off will make him invisible, expecting him to drive straight past.

'They never learn,' he thinks, as a burst of static precedes the response from control. There's no one available to assist for as traffic stop because there's been a nearby FATACC. He shrugs and decides to continue anyway, slowing down now as he reaches the farm and pulls into the yard, circling the area with his headlights as he looks for the hiding vehicle. Nothing. He stops in front of the only fully enclosed building, the headlights picking out that though the doors are closed, there is no padlock in place. Getting out of the car, he flicks his torch on and puts his hand on his taser. If it gets messy, he isn't going to take any chances. The door rolls open smoothly and his torch picks out an almost empty barn, the only vehicle a tractor tucked up against the side wall.

Pitbull returns to the car and decides to drive farther on down the lane. Maybe there's another entrance up ahead. The car has got to be here somewhere. Up ahead he sees a gated entrance and leans forward in the car, trying to pick out the edge of the gate, seeing rope tied around both gate and post. Jim sits back and tuts as he drives on, frustrated that he hasn't yet found the hiding place.

In the darkness behind him, the rope is lifted off the gate and the gate drawn wide open. Seconds later the black car bumps over the edge of the track and onto the road, silently sweeping back down the lane until it is past the farm.

Pitbull is about to give up on his search when a flash of a red brake light in his mirror catches his eye. He slams the BMW into reverse and heads back down the lane, swinging the car into the now-open gateway and then selecting drive and flooring the accelerator as soon as he's back on metalled track, pushing as fast as he can to catch up. But he's a long way behind.

Then, in the distance, he sees the long cones of headlights turning off the main road and into the lane and he grins. Another car is headed in and there are no passing places on the road.

Which means the two will meet in about half a minute.

12

Now Pitbull has him time to catch up. As he winds his way to the target vehicle, there's a flicker of brake lights and a brightening of the oncoming vehicle's headlights through the hedgerow. Soon it'll be all over. Travelling at speed now, he deftly balances the car through the bends and seconds later the black Tesla is in front of him.

The oncoming vehicle is stopped too, neither car wanting to reverse and solve the impasse.

As his car approaches the Tesla, Pitbull doesn't see the machete being pulled out from underneath the driver's seat and placed on the passenger seat, the handle nearest the driver. He doesn't see the driver shielding his eyes from the sharp intensity of the blue lights strobing behind him. He cannot see the black gloved fingers tapping the drive selector frantically as the police car draws to a halt.

Pitbull unclips his seatbelt and jumps out, pulling out his baton, anticipating he has a few seconds to smash the driver's window and stop the driver. His high-vis jacket flashes reflectively as he runs towards the window and draws back his arm, shouting somewhat unnecessarily:

"POLICE! STOP THE ENGINE."

At that moment the lights of the second vehicle start to shift backwards and the Tesla jerks forwards. Now Pitbull has to choose between chasing the vehicle on foot or running back to his car. He hesitates a moment, watching as the second vehicle continues to move backwards, slipping into the driveway of the farmhouse with the near empty barn.

The black car accelerates ferociously, leaving Pitbull hanging.

Fuck.

He knows he's not fast enough as he lumbers back to his own vehicle, fumbling with the keys and gets going. He ignores the driver waiting and races down the roadway to begin the chase. Yet it's a chase he knows he's lost. The car in front had been travelling at 100 mph for several seconds even before he got his own into second gear and though he can see the rear lights off in the distance, he knows there's a slip road and a junction a mile ahead on the main road and there is just no chance of making up the ground in time.

His right foot lifts and he slows down. No point calling for assistance; he knows that there is nothing in the area and that car could be anywhere in a few minutes. Worse yet, he can hear the stick he'll get from his colleagues for losing the car.

He decides to keep quiet for now. Experience has taught him that sometimes you get lucky in this job. Sometimes cars reappear when you least expect it and it will be easy enough to recognise it, at least before any repairs are carried out.

He cuts the blues and reduces his speed to the legal limit.

'Softly softly, catchee monkey,' he whispers out loud.

13

"You know that she was dead at the scene, of course," says Samza. There was some momentary response as you know but she never recovered. Since I'd already pronounced her dead, why don't you just leave it to me to sort out the paperwork?"

The ambulance pulls into the emergency bay at the hospital and comes to a stop. The doors to the back remained closed, one of the fluorescent lights flickering annoyingly as the paramedic sits still, thinking about what the doctor has just said. He rubs his hands over his face and looks up, acquiescence clear in his tired eyes.

"Are you sure? Actually I really need to get home, so it'd help."

"No problem at all. Leave it to me and I'll square it off. In this case, it doesn't really matter where she officially died, does it? She's not coming back either way."

The paramedic stands up, holds out a fist, acknowledging the bump as Samza smiles and nods.

"Thanks Doc, I owe you one."

"A pleasure. All in a night's work. Let's get her out of here, shall we?"

Twenty minutes later, the girl is on her way to the morgue and Samza is about to leave when a vibration in his pocket is accompanied by a muted ring tone. A quick glance up and down the hospital corridor and he lifts the handset to his ear, waiting for the caller to speak.

"How did it go?" asks the voice, without preamble.

"Okay. She's gone," he replies, "You should have hit her harder but I dealt with it."

"So I'll pick up the cash tomorrow then?"

"Yeah. Usual place. I'll text when I'm on my way."

Yet at the back of Samza's mind there is an itch.

Something isn't quite right.

14

He knows what it is; the man is a bit too keen to get the money.

Samza probes.

"How was the drive home?"

"Nothing I couldn't handle. Bit of blue interest but it's a fast car and it's gone now."

"Okay."

Samza disconnects and frowns. The man's words leave doubt. Something to handle means there is still a risk, somewhere. He'll have to address that at some point.

The doctor yawns. It's late and he's tired. He knows there'll be a lot more to deal with tomorrow but for now his work is done and he can go home. He starts walking away from the resus area and towards the entrance. Pulling out a different phone, a smartphone this time, he opens an app and orders a cab to take him back.

Five minutes later he is slumped in the back of a Prius, staring blankly out of the window as he tries to think of what the girl could have seen or done before he caught her.

She couldn't have done much. He'll check the cameras in the morning but she can only have been outside the window for a minute or so. And he was walking through the house at the time, so she won't have heard anything and simply won't have had the chance to do anything with it.

The taxi begins to turn into the road where Samza lives but is stopped by a police officer standing in front of a patrol car blocking the roadway. Samza pushes open the door of the taxi and waves at the young officer approaching the Prius.

"Hi Andy. Don't worry, he's just dropping me off."

Samza walks up the road, deliberately paying no attention to the crime scene personnel- he doesn't want to get involved in a conversation he hasn't had time to prepare for. He reaches his house and opens the front door, blinking in the bright lights that had been left on in the hallway when he ran out to attend to the girl. He shuts and locks the door, flicks the lights off and heads to the study at the back of the house, picking up a glass and a bottle of 25-year-old Macallan from the kitchen on the way.

He opens the whisky and sniffs appreciatively before he pours a good three fingers, placing the glass on the desk in front of the monitor. He drops back into the chair, picks up the glass and lifts his feet, crossing them as they rest on the corner of the desk. He takes a sip, savouring the warmth and the spicy heat, lingering over the flavours that swirl in his mouth and the fire that flickers as he swallows.

There is a framed, faded photograph on the shelf beside him and he reaches out to bring it down, placing it on the desk in front of him. He looks down at the woman in the photograph, takes another sip of the dark liquid and speaks out loud:

"I know it's been a while my darling, but it was worth the wait. Now you can rest in peace. For him, there'll be no peace. For him, now, the pain begins."

Samza smiles grimly and knocks back the remainder. Deeply satisfied he puts the glass down and makes his way to bed.

Today was a great day.

15

The lights of the cameras are shining directly into the face of Detective Inspector Winslaw. This is the part of the job he most dislikes; dealing with the press who almost inevitably will spin whatever he says to make things seem more tragic or more dangerous or downright incompetent (pick your own angle). The last time he had been in front of the cameras was after a particularly horrific stabbing when he had been appealing for witnesses. In any sane world, you wouldn't need to appeal. People would come forward just because. Not anymore. Society had changed a great deal in the last decade and he is glad that this is probably his last presser.

He finishes outlining the details of the car they are looking for, deliberately avoiding any mention of the aborted chase (much like that idiot Pitbull did before he was hauled in). He focusses instead on the last time the Tesla had been seen and is now asking if there are any questions. There are none of substance. Questions about motive, whether it was an accident or more sensationally 'did the girl know her killer?' were headline grabbers but useless when you are asking for help. Realistically, what can you ask when the police have just described a hit and run, explained the tragic loss of a family's daughter and appealed for help tracing a damaged car?

Finally, the lights dim and he can get back to his desk and plan for his retirement. He knows they won't find the car. It disappeared that night and hasn't been seen since. No-one is going to drive it on the public road any time soon and the people that might know where it is certainly won't be responding to the appeal. Still, it shows he's been doing something.

"Excuse me!"

He turns to look at a tall, skinny man, with wire frame glasses, pushing his way forcefully past the two reporters and heading straight for Winslaw. The DI nods and offers an outstretched hand as he recognises the girl's father, Dan Robinson. Offering his condolences once more, he suggests they move into an office to continue the discussion. Winslaw knows that distraught relatives rarely make police officers look good. They have barely got to the door of the office before the man launches into his questions.

"Look, I know you are looking for the car, but do you have any idea who did this? Or why?"

"It's impossible to say. It may be that they were drunk, not paying attention; on a phone or arguing with a girlfriend. Without witnesses there is really no way of knowing. Hence the appeal. Maybe she knew the people in the car?"

Robinson's face hardens as he picks up on the tone of the DI's comment.

"So now you're blaming the victim? How can you be so incompetently cruel?"

16

"I'm sorry. I didn't mean to cause offence. I'm just trying to find out what happened." Winslaw admits.

"She got killed that's what happened. And you need to find the killer."

Robinson drops his gaze, sinking into his slightly too large black overcoat as his eyes flicker across the table, searching his memory for any connection. "I can't remember seeing her anywhere near such a car," he says, "none of her friends or their families have one and she's never mentioned it."

"Could there be any other motive for someone to run her down?"

This time, Robinson looks directly at the Detective Inspector, anger flaring:

"Like what? She is a sixteen-year-old girl with her whole life ahead of her. Or at least she was. What on earth could she have been doing that would lead to being run over?"

"It's just that youngsters nowadays, you know, county lines and such like. Parents are often the last to know. Was she staying away from home when she was expected back? Missing school or anything?"

"No. She was doing well at school. She was just a normal..." Robinson's voice is trembling as he continues, "lovely... moody... teenager. What else can I say?"

"I'm sorry but I had to ask. Just one more thing for now though: Did she consider herself a, what do they call it, a Goth?"

"No. Why do you ask?"

"Well, it's just that Chloe was wearing a lot of black clothing the night she died."

Robinson's voice rises as he tries to understand what the detective is driving at.

"What the fuck has clothing to do with this anyway?"

"I really don't know," replies Winslaw slowly and gently. "We are just trying to work out why she was wearing black clothing at night like that. Do you know why she was in the road, at night, all in black? Have you any idea what she might have been running from?"

Chloe's father becomes angry.

"From the fucking car, obviously!"

Winslaw ignores the anger in the reply, giving the man a break under the circumstances.

"No, what I mean is, she was seen to be running even before the car started moving. So she could have been running away from something...or someone."

Robinson takes a deep breath and looks directly at Winslaw, tilting his head and frowning as he tries to understand: "What is wrong with you? Are you desperate for some ulterior motive or do you have some facts that support this crazy notion?

"No, Mr Robinson, I'm not and I don't. But my job is to look into all the possibilities here, especially when it involves the loss of such a young life."

Robinson nods in acceptance and Winslaw stands up, offering a card in case there is anything that the father wants to contact him about. Winslaw knows that appearing to be sympathetic and offering points of contact does very little to change the number of times he is contacted but it helps in the wider PR battle. And there is always the possibility that the man might remember something of use.

He isn't to know the father is deeply involved.

17

Winslaw sits at his desk and decides to ring Dr Samza. He has known him for some years, ever since the doctor moved into the area and agreed to work for the Police. Notwithstanding the words he has read in the official report, he wants to check for anything that might not have appeared in the text. Since a doctor at the scene can certify both death and cause of death, there is no need for a post-mortem.

"Hi doc, it's Rob Winslaw here."

"Hi Rob, how are you doing?"

"Not bad. Just finished an appeal for witnesses."

"How did it go?"

"Oh, you know, the usual routine and I'm not remotely hopeful we'll get anything on the accident. I'm pretty certain the car will never turn up. Unless we get a lucky hit on a speed camera somewhere but that's an increasingly faint chance now."

"How has the father been?"

"Pretty devastated to be honest. Into protecting the girl's memory now of course, which doesn't help much and which, in fact, is why I wanted to call you."

"Me? Sure. How can I help?"

"I'm just doing a final check through the details before the case goes cold- or before I retire anyway. Is there anything unusual that you can recall?"

There is a brief pause and Winslaw can hear the sound of Samza sucking in his lips as he thinks.

"Nothing unusual. Injuries entirely consistent with being run over at speed by a car. Took her up in the air and over the roof of the car, as I said before. She was probably gone the moment her head hit the windscreen. Would have left a hell of a dent in the car since it fractured her skull badly. I felt the back of her head as she was lying there and I can tell you it was quite a mess. No smell of drugs though and I didn't see any track marks or scarring of any sort that might indicate a history. Slight smell of alcohol maybe but I can't be sure."

"The paramedics said she was alive when they got there?"

"I know, it seemed that way. Last gasp of breath in the body, maybe. I think the paramedic wanted to save her but when you've seen a few of these, you just know when it's too bad for survival. I checked again in the ambulance and there was no sign of life at all."

"Okay. Look there is one other thing I haven't quite resolved. The father has asked for her phone back and I couldn't find any record of a phone in the paperwork or her effects. Did you happen to see it when you were attending to her?"

"Nope, no sign of a phone when I saw her. Given I was trying to save her life, I wouldn't have noticed if there was. If it was there, then your boys would have found it when they were checking the scene, wouldn't they?"

"Ordinarily, yes. And that's what's a bit odd. I mean, what teenager is ever out anywhere without a phone in their hand?"

"Good point," says Samza. "I'll take a look around myself when I get home if you like. See if it's been thrown out of her hand when she was hit. It could have gone anywhere, given the force of the impact. If I find it, I'll call you."

Samza ends the call and frowns. The phone. He should have looked. If it hadn't been for the ambulance...

Fuck.

18

2001

The doorbell rings and Arabella, as she advertises herself, checks her appearance in the mirror. Nothing too overt, just a tight-fitting T-shirt, no bra and short shorts, the kind of clothing that a young woman at home might be wearing on a hot summer's day, exactly as her advert described.

A deep breath and then she swings the door open, seeing the man who has arranged to meet her standing awkwardly on the doorstep. In truth, man is an optimistic description, given the gangly limbs and skinny frame that stand before her.

"Arabella?" he asks, his gaze flickering between the doorstep, the door frame and her.

"Of course," she replies, putting on a smile to ease his nervousness.

"Hi, I'm er...Andrew," says the boy-man, holding his hand out for a brief moment, uncertain as to whether he is going to shake hands or kiss her.

"Just come in, Andrew," says the girl, opening the door wide and standing to one side as he steps into the small, Victorian hallway.

"Go on upstairs," she tells him, "First door on the right."

The room he goes into is a simply furnished bedsit. It's clearly seen better days; the wallpaper is peeling at the corners of the ceilings, a musty smell mixes with the scent of a lighted incense stick and the plywood where the fireplace used to be is curling away from the wall. A small bay window, with a small, cheap white desk and folding chair in front of it, looks out over the street below. On the back wall a cheap double bed is placed up against the wall, clean white sheets and covers neatly arrayed on top. There is no other furniture apart from a small, empty bookcase placed between the bed and the window. Opposite there is a small sink with a cracked, mirrored cabinet above.

"Have you got the…er?" she asks.

"Oh yes," says Andrew, reaching into his pocket and pulling out five worn, ten-pound notes.

She takes the money, tells him to sit down on the bed, places the notes in a tin on top of the bookcase and then turns to close the curtains. This won't take long she tells herself, putting her arms on either side of her body and lifting her T-shirt up above her head, then turning round and looking at the boy-man. His embarrassment is palpable as his eyes look anywhere but at her breasts.

"Do you like what you see?" she asks, teasing him to look.

"Oh, er, yes, very much," he says. "You're quite beautiful."

"Why thank you," she says with mock modesty, "And you look very youthful, don't you? "How old are you? 18?"

"Er yes," says Andrew, unable to disguise the lie. Arabella shrugs as she inevitably accepts the deception and moves to stand right in front of him, looking at him as she slowly unbuttons her shorts, squeezes them over her hips and then drops them to the floor. All that is between his face and her body now is three inches of air and a cotton thong.

"Do you want me to undress you?" she asks softly.

"Oh er, I, I can manage," he says, putting his hands behind his head and pulling off his shirt and jumper in one movement. He drops them on the floor, nervously unbuttons his trousers and then awkwardly lifts his hips to allow her to pull them down and leave them on the floor.

She can sense how anxious he is. This might be really quick.

19

Arabella moves closer still, one leg on either side of him and pushes firmly on his chest, sending him backwards on the bed, his hands still held protectively in front of his underwear, as if he doesn't want to show the reaction he is now having.

Arabella knows what to do and it doesn't take long. A couple of minutes later he is pulling on his underwear and trousers. And she is grateful. She doesn't do this for pleasure; she needs the money to cover her rent and bills and to pay back the loan shark whose next payment is due tomorrow. Andrew, or whatever his name is, has provided a contribution.

She looks over at him, picking out a smile playing at the corners of his lips as he finishes dressing. Arabella pulls on a dressing gown and takes him to the front door and sees him out, closing it behind him and leaning up against the frame as she decides, again, that this is not what she wants to do anymore. In a week, she thinks, that'll be enough and she'll be out of debt. Then she can be free. Free to live a better life. Just a week, she tells herself as she climbs the stairs and goes into the bathroom to wash away the smells, the stickiness, the memory.

Yet the memory is the thing that won't wash away. Her memory of him will fade and almost disappear, a delicate strand of her subconscious keeping the knowledge of their meeting far from her mind, the faintest stain on her memory. For her, he was one of many.

For him, the encounter was more meaningful. And for him the memory will stay, kept alive for a few months as he relives his pleasure each night.

For him, she was one of one.

20

Present Day

It is almost dark as Joanna Robinson sits in her kitchen looking blankly through the back door and out into the garden, only vaguely aware of the rain running down the glass, not seeing the ash on the cigarette in her hand reaching the point where it will drop off. She doesn't notice it fall, just lifts her arm and takes another long drag, wincing slightly as tendrils of smoke linger at the edges of her eyes, then holds the inhaled smoke deep in her lungs before allowing it to snake out of her nostrils in a slow exhalation, as if keeping the poisonous gases in her lungs for longer would take her to her daughter more quickly, some sort of passive self-destruction.

In her mind she hears the sound of the backdoor handle squeaking as it is pushed down in the second before the door is thrust wide open and her daughter's voice is calling out that she's home. Asking what's for dinner. Slamming the door shut as she rushes through the kitchen and on to her own room. She hears the thump of footsteps on the stairs. The bathroom door. The flush, the walk. Drawers opening and shutting and then a delay, minutes passing until the footsteps descend and she returns to the kitchen, out of her school clothes and hungry. She hears the thirst for life in every movement. A life force that is strong and powerful and ever-present.

Except not today. nor tomorrow. Not for the rest of days.

The clock on the kitchen wall, a large red metal 1950s style clock that Chloe had insisted she buy, clicks as the long, slender second-hand moves, each slow second marked by a snick, a long pause before the next notch is reached and one more drop of life empties away.

Another drag and the heat from the burning nub brings her into the living present, forcing Jo to stub it out in the saucer beside her, reaching out automatically to pull another cigarette from the open packet on the table. A flick of flame and once more her lungs fill.

It's been two weeks since the funeral and time has yet to move. She is only dimly aware of the service as a foggy concoction of half-remembered faces, of vague platitudes, of pitying looks and sympathetic voices. She had heard one person talk about the funeral being some form of 'closure'. How stupid and irrelevant. As if some kind of arbitrary ritual can encapsulate the meaning of a bright young life, can mark a transition from motherhood to childlessness, can function as some kind of divider in life. Death is the real divider and the funeral feels like a means to formalise splitting her in two, taking her from happy and whole to broken and despairing, reinforcing the still-unaccepted fact that her daughter has been boxed up and incinerated, her earthly form destroyed, only memories and photographs remaining; painful memories of the past.

What hurts most though is the loss of what could have been and what should have been.

Yet Jo knows that this isn't the only painful thing she has to deal with. She knows she ought to talk to her husband about it but she doesn't know how. Even if she did know how, he wouldn't want her to. Not if it means the truth.

And now Chloe's death has made it impossible.

21

Robinson is walking, welcoming the sharp needles of rain pricking his face, soaking into his neck, chilling his face and hands. He relishes the momentary suffering it causes. He deserves it. He should have said something. He should have stopped her going out.

He hadn't been asleep. Joanne had been lying next to him, once more deep in a red-wine-fuelled sleep. He had, by then, given up trying to get her to change the pattern of the evenings. It always started reasonably, just a glass each at the start of the evening and the beginnings of a conversation. But he knew about her secret top-ups in the kitchen, the way conversations slipped into a tedious rhythm; questions asked and answered repeatedly. By ten o'clock she was a stranger; distant, disconnected and distracted. Tonight, he had wanted to talk about the empty bottles of wine that he had found at the back of a cupboard.

He had heard Chloe moving around in her bedroom; he had recognised the sound of her door scuffing the carpet as it opened. He knew she had been stealing down the stairs and going out.

He hadn't known what would happen, of course. How could he? But he could have prevented it. He could have stopped her going or at least slowed her down and then the car would have been in a different place and she would have survived. He could so easily have saved her life.

Now he is circling the roads around the house once more, passing through the simple suburban neighbourhood, along roads lined with family houses of all sizes, most set back from the kerb, some with larger gardens others less grand, but all typical examples of anodyne suburbia. These are places where kids grow, parents grow old, and houses are restored. And here he is, enviously passing the houses and their occupants, people for whom life hadn't changed one iota. Except, perhaps, if he acknowledges that there had been an inevitable sense of shock, some of it real, followed over the next few days by plenty of gossip about what had caused the loss of a young life. 'How could such a thing happen in this neighbourhood?' But nothing really changed for them.

Robinson knows about the stages of grief and he knows he's still in denial and anger, even though there's been a funeral. A funeral that passed in a fuzzy blur: a church service, a coffin and commiserations. Some may have known her life a bit perhaps, her friends and people at her school maybe, but no-one else, apart from Joanne, understands the reality of Chloe's life or the reality of her loss. And none of those people expressing sympathy have any real understanding of his loss; Being 'so very sorry' for him doesn't even begin to scratch the surface of his pain.

He hasn't been paying attention while he was walking. Now he looks up.

It was inevitable that he would end up here.

22

Robinson is standing right where the accident happened. Maybe it will bring him some closeness to her, some way to connect with her spirit.

But he is wrong. He feels nothing of the sort. The only feeling he has is confusion. How could a car be travelling at any kind of speed in this location at that time of night? What were the chances of her being in that place at that time and being hit by that car? He's not a mathematician but he knows the odds are incalculable.

So if it's not something that can happen naturally, then there was something else going on that night. And he remembers Winslaw's comment about Chloe running *before* the car started to move. The memory arrives even as he wants desperately to dismiss it. It would be easier to live with a random accident, having to accept that there are hardships in life and that tragedy can strike anyone randomly than to think that she had been deliberately mown down.

The police are showing no real interest in anything other than it being a terrible accident. A random hit and run theory. The driver just didn't see her when he started off.

Not that they've found the driver or the car. Apparently, a speeding car with a headlight out had been seen by a police car that evening but had disappeared and there was no trace. Not surprisingly they are saying there is nothing conclusive to connect it to Chloe's death. So the trail has gone cold and nothing is being done.

At least, he tells himself, the doctor was on the scene quickly. And if anything could have been done to save her, then he would have been there to do it.

Without thinking it through, Robinson strolls over to the doctor's front door, knocking loudly and standing back when he hears movement and sees a light come on in the hallway.

A chain rattles, a deadlock clicks and the door is pulled open, the doctor's suspicious face peering round the edge of the door, cautiously eyeing up the rain-soaked man, hair plastered to his head standing in front of him, his hands thrust deep into his coat pockets.

"Ah, Mr Robinson," says the doctor, recognition showing in his eyes. "I didn't know it was going to be you. Look, before you say anything, can I tell you just how sorry I am for your loss. Losing anyone is hard enough but to lose one's child, well..." He shrugs his shoulders and his head swings slowly from side to side as he seems to search for but cannot find better words. He opens the door a little wider albeit with one hand still holding onto the door lock, making a conversation easier but stopping short of inviting Robinson in.

"You know, there was nothing I could do, for her."

Robinson lifts a hand out of his pocket to wipe away the rain on his face, pushing back the hair on one side to clear his vision before he replies:

"I'm sure you did everything you could. Look, I don't know whether you can say but I just want to know. Was she awake when you got to her?

"No, I'm afraid she wasn't. I think she had gone by then."

"So she wasn't in pain?"

"No, I don't think so. With injuries like that, it's instant and painless. She won't have known anything about what happened, I can promise you that I made sure she wasn't suffering needlessly."

23

Robinson is relieved.

"Thank God for that. Did she say anything?"

"About what?" asks the doctor.

"Anything. About her mum? About me?"

"No, she couldn't I am afraid. She was already gone. I know it would have been comforting to have had a final message but I cannot give you that comfort. As I say though, she would have gone without feeling much pain."

"I thought you said she didn't feel any."

"No, she p-r-obably didn't. But you can never be absolutely certain with these things you know. Even if she had felt anything, there is no point torturing yourself with the knowledge that she suffered. If she had, it would have been only for a very short while. I'm certain of that. And even then, the shock can sometimes protect the body from pain with accidents that severe."

"That's some comfort, I suppose."

"I hope it is," says the doctor, his tone indicating he has more to say. He waits by the door and as Robinson begins to thank him, the doctor interrupts with a question:

"Look, I can't help but wonder why she was outside at that time of night. And dressed in all black clothing. Do you have any idea what she had been doing before the accident?"

Robinson shakes his head: "I have no idea. And don't they all wear black anyway?"

"Yes, I suppose they do," says the doctor.

Robinson turns to walk away but stops and looks back; "Did you perhaps pick up her phone? She was never without it."

"No. Why do you ask?"

"I don't know. Maybe it would have had something in it, anything really, that might explain her actions."

"I see. Sadly not."

"Thanks for your help and thanks again for all you did for Chloe."

"Oh, I was glad to do it, however little it might have been."

As he walks away, Robinson tries to shake a feeling that is just discernible, a sense of something wrong that he should pay attention to but which is so vague that it is out of his mind's grasp the moment it appears. He can't face going home yet. He walks back to the roadway, scanning subconsciously, looking for a phone he knows he won't find. It must still be indoors somewhere. Most likely in her room. And that's where the problem lay. He can't face going in there. He can cope with the rest of the house but hasn't been in her room since the hit and run. It hurts too much.

At least he now knows that Chloe didn't suffer. It might help Joanne, he tells himself, even though he suspects that nothing can really help her.

Not even him.

24

Standing in the kitchen, Robinson steels himself.

"I'm going to check her room."

"You're wasting your time," says Joanne.

"What do you mean?"

"Nothing in there to find. No mystery to solve."

He doesn't respond. He knows there is nothing he can say. The two of them haven't spoken to each other since yesterday when he returned home, both of them living in a kind of suspended animation. Alive but not in.

"I don't want her room changed," she adds.

"I'll be careful."

Joanne shrugs and takes another drag of her cigarette, directing the exhaled smoke downwards as she watches him go upstairs. She listens to the sound of the carpet scraping under the door and the footsteps on the carpet. If only they were *her* footsteps. But they are not.

Upstairs, Robinson stands still, his hands in his hair as he looks uselessly at the detritus of a teenage girl's room; fading pink walls and white furniture with a bed along the wall to the right and a wardrobe, chest of drawers and small desk against the wall to the left; deep red curtains drawn across the window, cutting out the streetlight. They had been promising to redecorate for months but he just hadn't got round to buying the paint.

There are clothes lying on the single bed, several pairs of shoes left on the floor in front of the wardrobe and bits of make-up and jewellery on the chest of drawers. He can see her wearing each item, see her feet in the shoes and her body in the clothes. He closes his eyes for a moment and takes a deep breath, trying to hold back the sea of emotion. Think, he tells himself. No tears. Just think about finding answers. What do you see? What does the room tell you?

Clearly the clothes show the signs of a girl trying to decide what to wear. And no time to put things back. No sign of having thought through what she would do. Just a rush. The laptop is closed so that was done before she started getting ready to go out. Perhaps the answer is there. About to step over to the desk he sees the empty lead hanging down. The charger without the phone. She *had* taken it with her.

He sits at the chair by the desk and opens the small drawer underneath. Looking for a diary or a journal, not really thinking through that most of a young girl's life is lived on Instagram and Facebook. Instead, what he finds is an old phone with a smashed screen, the first phone he had bought her, a packet of tobacco and some cigarette papers. And a small plastic bag with two round pills inside, embossed with the outline of some kind of creature. Probably ecstasy, he thinks, pushing aside the notion that she might have been dealing rather than experimenting. There is a faint smell too. A familiar sweet smell that he had always thought was confined to his wife's 'jewellery' box.

Nothing though, that would shed any real light on why she had been out.

Robinson opens the computer and sees the password dialog box. He knows this is going to be difficult. Chloe was always going on about how easy passwords were to guess. So he imagines she will have been careful with her own. He tries her name and year of birth; Password1234 (just in case), Password 4321, her middle name, their only dog's name, her grandmother's name, her grandfather, all with a number from 1 to 10 after it and before it. Then he stops. He knows he won't guess it.

There are some things teenagers just don't want their parents to know.

25

Robinson stares blankly at the screen. Maybe he needs password cracking software. But even if he can find some, he doesn't know how he'll get it onto the computer, except somehow through a thumb drive, he supposes. Maybe there'll be a shop he can take it to, but he hesitates. He doesn't want a stranger going through the computer, especially when he doesn't know what's on it. A stranger might talk about what he sees.

For now though, Robinson can do nothing. He turns in the chair and looks around the room. No clues. He lifts the bed cover and looks under the bed. Nothing unusual, just plastic boxes with old clothes in. And a smaller cardboard box. His heart starts to beat faster as he reaches in and pulls the box towards him, taking a deep breath as he unfolds the interwoven leaves of the top of the box. Inside there are photos. And cards. From her last birthday. Polaroids from the Christmas before last, when her uncle had given her a Polaroid camera and she had used up both boxes of film that day. He sorts through the photos she had taken, lingering over the one she took of her mother from a silly angle, and smiles at the sight of one of him with a Christmas hat on and fast asleep in a chair, the blurry image of the television in the background.

And then he sees the photo that breaks him. It is Chloe, in front of a mirror, taking a polaroid selfie, her bright shining eyes exuding so much vitality, so much fun, so much life. He lies down on the bed now, clutching the selfie and breathing in the faint scent of her on the pillow and the tears come.

26

It's early in the morning when the kitchen light flickers on and Samza fills the kettle. After a broken night's sleep, he'd like a whisky but he has work to do and he knows it won't just be one glass. And he cannot afford to make a mistake. Not if he wants to live.

Taking his freshly made tea with him, he steps into the study at the back of the house, looking at the layout of the room. The desk is not quite square on, which is exactly as he left it, and, moving closer, he checks that the edge of the handwritten sheet in front of the monitor lines up exactly parallel to the window. Nothing has changed. He doesn't actually expect there to be any movement; nobody else is there to touch his papers. But he needs to know if it ever does happen.

His mug is placed on the windowsill. He disconnects the laptop on the table; it's full of the things you'd expect to find on a police doctor's laptop- dull-sounding papers, copies of medical journals, expenses. It's not what he wants.

He opens the bottom desk drawer and reaches underneath the papers that fill it. His hands grasp metal and he retrieves his second laptop. Placing it onto the desk, he connects it up and the computer kicks into life. Once the VPN and router have been started, he can begin his work. He remembers when he started in medicine many records were paper based. Now you can get access to patient histories and full medical records with the click of a mouse. Which is useful for people engaged in providing the best care possible. It is also useful to those who want to access data for other purposes. Once you know how the system works, you can sell that access. Samza had accepted a sizeable sum of money in exchange for the opportunity to support a fledgling medical start up with relevant information, information they wouldn't normally be able to see. Information they can change.

This helps them avoid the rigorous systems that, in their words, stultify the development of innovative companies. For his access payment, all he has to do is change a word here, make a deletion there, alter symptoms or a cause of death. Nothing that would actually change a patient's personal outcome, not in the immediate term anyway.

He had also agreed to check medical histories for named individuals, to look for people with certain illnesses, to find the terminally ill. He deliberately didn't ask why he had been asked to do this, even if he had a pretty good idea. It was best to be able to say he had no knowledge. His only convictable crime is providing data. And a spell in jail or a fine wouldn't be that bad. He had been told that in those circumstances silence would be safest. Talking would be very dangerous.

He knows to take the threats seriously.

27

Now that he is logged on, he checks the list on his screen and begins work. He reviews the details on the death certificate for a patient he had seen earlier. It had been a young boy, aged 16. The cause of death had been given as anaphylactic shock. That much was true. But now he is going to erase the results of the post-mortem tests that had shown traces of heroin and ketamine in her body, as well as an initial dose of a yet to be announced, experimental psychoactive drug. It isn't certain that it had contributed to the boy's death- the peanut oil had done that all on its own- but it certainly wouldn't be helpful for a record to remain if someone went looking for a reason behind his recklessness.

Samza is distracted. And it's not the work causing it. It's the phone. He needs to ensure there is nothing on it that might incriminate him in some way. He'll have to find it. Clearly it's not at the girls home. And it won't be in the roadway. The police would have found it. Which means it has to be somewhere on his property. Instinctively he looks up at the window and the night outside, trying to replay the memory of movement that had triggered his check the night the girl died. She'd had it in her hand at that point.

So between the time he saw her, made the call and she ran out, she must have stashed the phone.

Which leaves only one question for now.
Where?

28

It is still dark outside as the doctor steps out of his back door. The garden is of a good size, bordered by hedges, trees and fences. The hedges are evergreen but elsewhere leaves have fallen and all that is left are the dark lines of branches and twigs against the pale blue sky. It's cold. Very cold. His breath forms a large cloud of vapour as he stands outside the window. There are a number of places she could have hidden it so he needs to be methodical.

The lights from the house provide light to search with but they also make him visible to others. Even though it's his own garden, a neighbour looking out of a window will certainly question why he is creeping around the garden this early. So he picks up a garden fork for cover and begins his search, starting at the left side and then slowly working his way through every inch of the garden, looking for disturbed earth, bits of fabric, anything that would help him see where she had been. Frustratedly, he reminds himself that she could have deliberately left the phone anywhere. Which means looking under the wheelbarrow, beneath the bins, lifting out the sealed dustbin bags in case it had been dropped down the side. Nothing. He walks slowly around the shed, pushing his fingers into every gap he can find beneath the wooden structure. No joy. He even checks the guttering of the garage, stretching up and dipping his hand onto the icy cold frost lining the plastic strips. Nothing.

An hour later and he still hasn't found anything. He stands, hands on hips, talking out loud. Now girl, where would you have put it? And yet, he questions, would she have had the nous to hide it at all? She's scared, trying to hide and get away. Is it feasible for her to have really decided to hide the evidence? Unlikely. But not impossible.

Fuck.

Reluctantly he goes back to the bins and checks for any rips in the bags. None. But even as he doubts the possibility of her putting a phone in through the tightly tied binbags he knows there is only one thing to do. Screwing up his face, he pulls at the plastic. Five minutes later he's had enough, packing up what's left into new plastic bags and hurrying indoors to warm up and get a hot coffee.

Perhaps then, he tells himself as he is grinding fresh coffee, perhaps he's in the clear after all. The phone is definitively not hidden in the garden. Maybe it was never there; yet even as the thought passes through his mind, he doesn't believe it.

He takes the coffee upstairs and heads for the shower. Whatever else is going on, he has a surgery to take in forty-five minutes.

The hot water runs down his face and body, cutting through the cold and restoring his fingers and feet to life. He smiles as he squirts some shampoo in his hands and begins to rub his hair, the sensation reminding him of the grip of his fingers on her face, the tips sensing the hair of her scalp as his hold tightened, the feel of the many strands settling beneath his fingers as he pulled her head upwards and then slackened as he thrust downwards.

He wants to tell Robinson all about it. About the feel. The fear. The last, confused, bewildered look she gave him. The split-second understanding in her eyes that he was going to take her life away and she was utterly powerless to intervene. And she will never be able to understand why; never able to understand why she had to die.

But he is going to bide his time. There'll be a perfect time to talk.

Just not yet.

29

Joanne is awake. As she has been for hours. She wasn't awake when her daughter needed her to be, but she is awake now. She rolls her head towards the bedside clock once more. It is still 3.39 am. Whatever the time, she knows she should have been more convincing. Maybe told the truth. It might have stopped Chloe going round to see Samza. Jo knows that's why she had been in the road. She had been on her way to see the doctor.

Joanne still doesn't know whether she had made it that far. Whether she had spoken to Samza. Or what he had said to her.

But she can't do anything about it yet. It's too soon, way too soon.

She sighs and turns back to face her sleeping husband. Maybe she should have taken a pill too. At least her mind would be still for a few moments, taking her away from the thoughts are spinning around inside her mind, on a loop. The lies she had told Chloe, the weak attempt to keep the truth away; the look Chloe had given her, the look that said 'I have heard the words and know you are lying to me.'

Chloe had been waiting for her in the lounge that day; lying on the worn blue velvet sofa, wearing blue-checked pyjama bottoms and a pale pink T-shirt with a black, mirror-print logo that reads: "It's not this shirt that is inside out. It's you!", some sort of never-ending reality TV programme playing on the screen in the corner.

The first words Chloe had spoken were softly said but carried a sharp edge, an anger seeping into the phrasing: "Go on then."

Joanne wasn't quite sure what was happening.

"Go on then what?"

"Nothing."

"So have you been here all day?" she asked her daughter, regretting the implied criticism in the question the moment the words came out of her mouth. Chloe replied, her chin jutting forward as she responded:

"No-o-o. And what if I had been?"

Joanne decided to try another tack by asking what she was watching.

"You don't really want to know, do you?"

There was no point waiting. Might as well tackle it.

"Okay Chloe, what's up?"

"Nothing."

Joanne lifted the remote control and pointed it at the TV.

"Right, now that's off you can talk to me. What's up?"

"I don't really think you need me to tell you, do you?"

"I think I do. What's up? What have you done?"

"It's not me," said Chloe.

"So it's me then, is it?"

"I don't know. Maybe. Maybe you should just ask *him*."

"Eh?"

"You know. How can you not know, for fuck's sake? Oops, sorry for the clue."

Joanne didn't want to take the bait. Whatever she said would inevitably sound defensive. Even if there was nothing to defend.

"Well, I'm going to go upstairs and have a long bath. It's been quite a day and I don't have the patience for this now."

She was almost out of the room when she heard Chloe's words.

"Maybe Dad will."

30

Lying in the bath, beneath a thick layer of foam, Joanne pondered her next move. At least now she knew for sure what Chloe thinks is going on. And that wasn't entirely helpful. Because if she tells her she isn't having an affair, she may not believe it. And she'd have to tell her something else. If not the truth, at least something credible and feasible.

Moments later she had an answer. Something close enough to true but not enough for the things to unravel. She would soon see if it worked.

"Can we have a civilised conversation now?" she had asked, walking once more into the lounge. Her daughter had barely moved.

Chloe shrugged; her eyes still focussed on the TV; her way of saying go on.

"I imagine you were referring to my recent visits to Dr Samza, earlier on?" asked Joanne.

"Duh!"

"Well, you may as well know he is thinking about building an extension to his property and he wanted my advice."

"Except you're not a builder."

"No, I am not. But I do work in the planning department and it's helpful to know what mood the planners are in before barrelling in with a scheme."

"I think he was probably more interested in the mood you were in."

"Chloe, cut it out. I'm not in any way involved with Dr Samza and it really pisses me off that you think so. I love your father and I would never behave like that."

Joanne knew that this wasn't entirely true but no need to tell Chloe that.

"Whatever."

"Now get off that sofa and tidy the place up a bit will you, before your father gets home."

*

"What's wrong with her?" asked Robinson after dinner that night.

"Nothing. Teenage years obviously."

"It's just that a couple of times during the meal she looked up at me and I couldn't work out what the look meant."

"I'm not sure I'll be able to explain any of that," she said. "Sometimes there doesn't actually have to be anything wrong, you know. The mood is the mood, even if there is no reason."

"I know. I think I might go and see if she's alright."

"Have you forgotten the last time you tried that?"

"Fair point. Maybe I'll just leave it. If there is anything, she'll say it in her own good time."

Robinson didn't know then that her own good time was so limited.

31

Present Day

The man in the computer shop was everything you'd expect. Beanie, spectacles, wrinkled clothes, sharp eyes.

"Can you get in then?" asks Robinson.

Beanie rolls his eyes.

"I can, obviously. Nothing is impregnable but I don't know that I should. Is it yours?"

"Yes."

"Really? With stickers like that on it?"

Robinson looks away. He knew it would be like this the moment he set foot inside the shop. If you could call it that. It is more like a computer junk store than a well-organised repair shop. Yet that was the very reason he chose it. He wants to see what was on her laptop without it being reported anywhere; he wants the password and nothing more.

"It was my daughter's."

Recognition is slowly dawning in the face of the geek:

"I know who you are. I seen your picture. You're the dad of that hit and run girl."

For a split-second Robinson considers explaining that her name was Chloe and she wasn't the hit and run girl. She was the girl who was murdered. But he knows it will be pointless. And he's regretting coming in here now, because geek boy will tell people all about his visit.

"Look, just find the password for me, will you?"

"Sure. Do you want to come back tomorrow and pick it up?"

"No. I don't. I don't want you ghoulishly rummaging through the contents while I'm gone. I'll wait."

"Could be quite a while," says the geek, pursing his lips.

Robinson answers by moving a keyboard from a battered old chair and sitting down, folding his arms.

"Okay," says the geek, disappointment in his voice. "But it is extra for 'as you wait' service."

"Don't push it."

Nineteen minutes later the geek lets out a 'sick' and turns to look at Robinson.

"Done. Want to know what it was?"

"Go on then."

"Specialksupply".

He frowns. She hated Special K. Always preferred cornflakes. Why would she have...?"

His thoughts are interrupted by the crowing of the geek.

"You would never have broken it," smiles the geek. "That's fifty quid please."

Robinson hands over the money and takes the laptop, closing it and then reopening it to test the password before leaving.

The next steps need to be taken somewhere private.

32

Robinson rubs his eyes and then his face with his hands. This is really challenging. Not intellectually but emotionally. Every page, every photo contains a reminder of how lovely and full of life she was. He can hear her words in the schoolwork that is in her word programme. But that's not the bit that he needs.

He opens her email account and lets the computer autofill the password, taking a deep breath and then pressing the enter key.

What he sees is quite shocking. It's definitely her email account but there are no emails. None. Not one in her inbox and there are no folders. Nowhere that might store information that might be in any way helpful.

Fuck.

Robinson pushes back from the desk and closes his eyes, trying to remember something that is sitting at the edge of his memory. He had a discussion with her a while ago about her phone obsession and remembers her talking about Instagram.

Presumably the computer will remember her log in for Instagram too. He opens the site and clicks log in. A few seconds later he is in. Except it's not her account. It's someone called Stormb387. Then he recognises the photo. She's changed it somewhat, altered contrast and colour, but it's Chloe. He just knows.

He spends half an hour going through the feed, looking at messages she has received, trying to follow likes and look at who she's been talking with. Until he cannot cope with it all any longer. The combination of teen-speak, new technology and the near indecipherability of some of her posts cause him to shake his head in both fatigue and wonder. He had no idea. No idea that this was happening nor that he would understand so little of it. How could his little daughter have grown so far apart from him? Or perhaps a better question was how could he have paid so little attention to the new technologies and what his daughter had been saying and doing online? Fortunately, there was nothing on there (that he understood) that would indicate anything unpleasant happening, but a chill runs down his spine as he realises the things that might have been happening while he had no idea.

But whatever might, or might not, have happened, he still needs to find answers to the only question that really matters. Why was she killed? He keeps scrolling through for clues. But there's nothing to indicate anything criminal nor anything that might put her at risk. No sign of a stalker or groomer. The answer isn't in her social media stalker then. But who did kill her?

He knows he needs to talk to Jo about it really. Mother and daughter were naturally much closer than he was to Chloe and there were times when he sensed they were in on secrets that he would never know. Correction. He knew there were secrets.

But he doesn't have any idea how on earth he might open up that line of conversation. How do you ask a grieving mother to recall intimate conversations with her daughter? Especially when she'll never be able to have those conversations again. And how do you get past the barrier that has formed around Joanne, leaving her in a near catatonic state that allows no room for any reaction? Worse than that, he knows that even if he does manage to break through, she will insist that it doesn't matter anymore, that if Chloe had taken her into her confidence, then it should stay secret. Robinson rubs his hands across his face, lightly at first but then harder as he realises how hard this is going to be.

He doesn't realise that it's going to be even harder when he finds out that it wasn't only Chloe with secrets.

33

It's been bugging him all day. Maybe he needs to look again. More closely. More carefully. It means opening up the computer and seeing her wallpaper screen once more and looking at the picture of her in a helicopter smiling with all the joy in the world. Taken when they went on holiday in Canada and as they flew around Grouse Mountain near Vancouver. It was her twelfth birthday, and so before the teenage years kicked in and while childhood still allowed for unbridled joy and happiness. She is beaming broadly, hair long and blonde beneath a set of grey headphones, and he has never seen her so happy. Just seeing it tears at his insides.

He enters the password and starts to look through more files, fighting the deepening sense of anguish that is seeping into his feelings. Wherever he looks, whatever he sees, it just stings more, making the loss keener. Ten minutes, he decides, He'll give it ten minutes.

An hour later and he realises that he has to stop. It's hopeless. He knows he's barely scratched the surface. It'll take hours to go through all the material in there and his heart tells him he won't find anything more. Just a line into the life of his own special daughter. He wants to explore her world and yet he doesn't want to look anymore. Clinging to her isn't going to help him deal with it. And letting her go is impossible to accept. Maybe once he's found the reason for her death, he can let it go.

Maybe.

He is about to log off when he remembers the thing that's been bugging him. It was the argument that had lodged it in his memory. He and Joanne had disagreed over the idea that they were invading her privacy; a notion that was eventually overridden by the more practical issues of wanting to know where she was. And they had decided to pitch the idea as if it were just a means of helping her to know where it was if she ever lost it or had it stolen. When the two of them had suggested it, Chloe had just laughed. "That app is already in there," she chuckled: "It's called 'Find my phone' and we *all* know that 'find my phone' means 'find my daughter'!"

So she had left it still on the phone. Except of course, after all this time, the battery will certainly be dead, so the thing is almost certainly useless. But at least it would show the last known location. If only he knew how to do it.

Twenty minutes later he finds it.

Yet it makes no sense. He couldn't understand why it would be there. Chloe had been in the road when she died. Sure, it might have been thrown out of her hand, but it wouldn't be far away. Or she might, just might have left it at home when she had gone out. Why would the phone end up anywhere else, apart from with her? But at least he knows where to start if he is to find the answer.

The phone was last shown near to home. He zooms in.

It takes him ten seconds to be certain where the phone has been.

It's going to take a little longer to find out why someone is lying about it.

34

Robinson rubs his eyes and decides he might as well get up now. As he stands, he looks out of the bedroom window. From here he can see the house. In summer there'd be no chance but with bare branches he can clearly see Samza's property.

He's been standing here for some time now. It started as a quick look but each moment stretches into one more minute and now he's been watching for over an hour.

A thought has passed through his mind several times now and though he wants to dismiss it out of hand, he knows it is perfectly plausible. Chloe was young. Impressionable. Naïve. And Samza is a doctor. Not without charm. And for some reason, Samza didn't look Robinson full in the eye when they last spoke. No, it can't be that.

Can it?

Then he sees movement. A shadow sweeps across the front room window and he knows his man is there. He was the last person to see Chloe alive and Robinson still has questions to ask. Ideally, he would have had a chance to look around the house before confronting the man, looking for any more evidence of Chloe having been there.

Now there is movement in the back garden. He can see Samza moving along the flowerbeds at the very back of his garden, a long wooden pole in his hand as he searches the deepest recesses of the hedge. Slowly, he moves around the perimeter, disappearing from sight as he reaches the side nearest the front fence, just the top of the hoe appearing intermittently.

Then the gate opens.

The doctor appears and begins the same search of the front garden.

Robinson decides now is the time to act. He goes downstairs, slipping on shoes and a jacket and making his way over to the doctor's house. He is a bit surprised to find no sign of the man, the house looking for all the world as if it is empty. Undeterred, he strides up to the front door and bangs loudly, stepping back to wait for a response.

There isn't one.

Robinson steps up to the door and lifts himself up on his toes, trying to peer through the glass panel that sits at the top of the door. He can make out the hallway and the stairs, empty and still. Fuck. He must have missed the man. He is slipping back down to his heels when he spots it. A dark mass.

He jumps up on his toes to look again. There, in the doorway on the wall to his right, he can see hair.

Why isn't the man answering?

Robinson steps back and swings his arm hard, bringing his hand down with a thunderous bang on the door. A noise he repeats several times.

Still no response.

He tries again, this time shouting out the doctor's name as he does so.

"Come on, open the fucking door, man! I can see you in there."

35

Next to the doorway, Samza stays still, hoping it's a bluff. He knows he isn't well hidden but hoping it is just good enough. It's too soon to talk to Robinson again. He needs time, he needs the right circumstances. The doctor stays put, waiting for Robinson to go, but it is becoming increasingly apparent that he won't leave anytime soon. Which means Samza needs to find a way to deal with the man. And there's only one real approach he can adopt: Attack.

Outside, running out of patience, Robinson resumes his banging and threatens to smash the 'fucking door down', well aware that to judge by the movement he feels beneath his fist, he is half-way to succeeding.

Then the locks turn and the door is yanked open by an angry Samza.

"What the fuck do you think you're doing?" he shouts, flecks of spittle shooting from his mouth as he steps forward and gets up into Robinson's face. Shocked by the venom, Robinson recoils.

"I KNOW YOU ARE A GRIEVING FATHER BUT THAT DOES NOT GIVE YOU THE RIGHT TO COME ROUND TO MY HOUSE SHOUTING ABUSE! I WAS

THE MAN WHO TRIED TO SAVE YOUR NOSEY FUCKING DAUGHTER! SHOW SOME FUCKING RESPECT."

Taken aback, Robinson splutters "Look, I'm sorry but..."

"I should fucking think so! Now what do you want?"

Suddenly Robinson isn't so sure. He wishes he wishes he had thought it through before piling in.

"I just, I just wanted to know if there was anything else that she said? Anything that might have explained the accident?"

The hardness in Samza's face eases as he repeats what he has already said previously about the incident.

"It's just that I am trying to find answers, you know?" says Robinson, "I was hoping that you'd maybe found her phone since this was the last place that it registered."

This time, Samza reaches out his hand, touching Robinson's arm and speaking softly.

"It may have seemed that way, but technology isn't always perfectly reliable. She could just have been walking near my home."

"Yes, but it showed up as being at your home *after* the accident!"

The doctor waits a few seconds before responding, letting the words hang in the air before his eyebrows knit together and he speaks in a softer tone:

"Look, the police searched and found nothing, so I don't know what more to say."

Robinson's shoulders slump.

"I don't really know why the phone matters, he says, "it's only a phone after all. I suppose I'm just hoping there's something to tell me she didn't just die for no reason."

Samza nods.

"I know how difficult this is. I've seen it many times before. Sometimes, there just are no reasons. I'm really sorry for your loss."

He turns to go back inside, pausing at the door as he thinks, then adds a comment:

"I know you are upset, but please don't come round to my house again. If you want to talk, I'm happy to do so, but at the surgery. I'll tell the receptionist to make sure you can always get an appointment. And once again, I am deeply sorry for your loss."

The door closes and it doesn't register at first. There. On the table in the hall.

It's a phone.

A phone with the same cover as Chloe's.

36

The door closes and Samza breathes a long sigh of relief. He's got rid of the man and, more importantly, he's got the phone. He picks it up and walks through to his study, checking the connector and plugging it into his computer directly. A few minutes work and he's in.

All the usual apps. He starts with Instagram. And before long he's bored with photos of me, me, me. And the messages are just what you'd expect of a teenage girl. Nothing unusual. Yet this will provide him with opportunity. A chance to use her own accounts to backdate some posts, change photographs and inject a little doubt. Not too much. Just enough for someone to see the content if necessary but not to go looking for the tracking data. He keeps searching. The trouble is he is looking for something but he doesn't really know what. So he'll have to check everything.

He goes through WhatsApp, scrolling through streams of teen consciousness. Useful information sure. An insight into her mind. Or more accurately, a view of the myriad mini-crises that this girl seemed to have gone through.

He's almost given up when he remembers to look at the raw photos. Photos she has taken but not posted. And he's glad he has.

There's a video. Of him.

He's not looking at the camera. The shots were taken from outside the study and show him looking at the monitor. He pinches and opens his thumbs on the phone, focussing in on the content of the monitor in front of him. He doubts she will have put it together. Certainly not from that shot. It doesn't show who the details are about, nor what he was doing with them. Could easily be a snap of him just working from home and checking medical notes.

He knows whose file was up on the screen, of course. Not many people have that kind of drug history and are still working in socially important roles.

Still, nothing too worrying there. He flicks back through time and sees several shots of the study window and blurry snaps.

Before those there are other, different, photos. Photos of his house. From a distance and from an elevated position but definitely pictures of his house. Taken a couple of weeks ago. Probably the last time there had been a truly sunny day. He could tell it was early afternoon, the light already beginning to fade. There was a figure at his front door. He knew who it was.

But Chloe had been watching. Taking pictures. He scrolled back, looking for more but finding nothing of significance. There was nothing incriminating on there. Nothing at all. So why had she been lurking outside then? Why was she taking photos of his house and then his study? For a moment, he wishes he hadn't had taken her out so swiftly. Yet there had been no time.

And of course, it had given him the result that he wanted.

He's not sure what to do with the phone though. He can ditch it but experience tells him that sometimes it's the loose ends that keep the police interested. And a lost teenage phone is a loose end.

He'll drop it in the girl's garden later. Once he's wiped his prints of course. Or better yet, smeared all the prints to avoid suspicion.

For now though, there is work to be done.

37

Robinson shuts the door softly behind him, feeling the heavy silence as soon as he enters. While he takes his shoes off and hangs his coat up, he is thinking about his encounter with the doctor. He knows that he shouldn't have gone over there with that amount of anger. It wasn't the doctor he was angry with of course; the man had tried to save his daughter even when she had received catastrophic injuries. It hadn't been Samza's fault. And Robinson, of all people, knows that accidents could happen. But there had been no need for the doctor to be rude about Chloe. It's true she was inquisitive but he didn't have to call refer to her as 'fucking nosey'.

Gingerly, he opens the door to the front room. She is there of course; sitting in the armchair, cigarette in hand, looking straight ahead, showing no sign of his having entered. There is a tendril of smoke curling up from the edge of her mouth, rising to the side of a nostril, past her unblinking eyes and dissipating in the air above.

Robinson sits down on the sofa, grunting as he leans back into the cushion. She doesn't respond. No questions; no comments.

She doesn't even turn her head, just robotically lifts the cigarette, inhaling and exhaling automatically.

He wants to talk. He wants to reach her. But he doesn't know how.

Sighing he leans forward, shifting his weight and pushing up.

"Do you want a tea?" he asks, walking out to the kitchen, returning with two mugs of tea which he sets down on the table.

"Where have you been?" asks Joanne.

"Making tea."

"I meant before that."

"Just to talk to the doctor." He hopes the simplicity of his reply will take the sting out of her response. He is wrong.

"I don't know why you're wasting your time," says Jo without moving. "She's gone and she isn't coming back.

"You think I don't fucking know that?"

This time she turns, facing him directly as she spits out another question: "Then why the hell are you going over to his house. It's not going to help. Just leave him alone, will you?"

Robinson is about to respond but he stops himself. There's no point going on. He doesn't have any arguments to explain why he is so fixated on the doctor, except of course for the phone and even then, he doesn't actually know the doctor has *her* phone.

"Whatever you say. But I still think there is something really wrong about that doctor."

"Oh, don't be stupid. He's a bloody doctor. The only thing wrong is that he didn't have you sectioned."

Robinson gives up. He won't win. He leaves the room to get a drink. It's only when he reaches the kitchen that the thought occurs to him.

Why is she so defensive of the doctor?

38

September 2000

A torrent of water is lashing the front of the house, pouring out over the guttering and splattering on the ground below. There is a heavy drum roll of thunder from a leaden sky, a sky that has blackened sharply, plunging the room into darkness.

Beneath the bed covers, Peter and Emma are cuddling, her head in the crook of his shoulder, his arm around her shoulders, her leg draped over his as she idly runs her fingers across his chest. Their breathing has settled now, a feeling of well-being and peace running through both of their sated bodies, a physical and emotional heat soothing them after the intensity of their love-making.

They are in Emma's room. Her parents have gone away for the weekend and she has told them she would be studying for her 'A'-levels. She had told them that she might have one of her friends round to watch a movie and have a takeaway. She implied, but didn't specify for sure, that the friend would be her best friend. A best friend who had been primed to confirm all the relevant details if asked, however innocently, buy an inquisitive mother when next she visited. But her friend had been busy with her own boyfriend and she hadn't made an appearance. The secret was safe.

Or that's what she thought. Her mother was more discreet and sensitive than Emma gave her credit for: She had seen the changes in her daughter's behaviour; the whispered phone calls; the distant looks; the smiles. She had even known what had happened the morning after her daughter had first had sex; she recognised the scale of blushing when an article on teenage sex had run on morning TV that day. But she had said nothing, wanting to protect her child's transition into a woman, allowing the secrecies and the omissions, helping to elide truth and pretence.

She wouldn't tell the girl's father. He wouldn't understand and wouldn't know how to respond. Most likely he'd make things more difficult than they already were for a young woman. And she didn't tell him because she knew the name of the boy Emma was seeing. And when it came to that boy, her husband would have taken the populist view.

So she had said nothing when they were planning a weekend away; convincing him that his daughter was old enough and sensible enough to be perfectly safe on her own at home, especially with her best friend coming round. For his part, he had given her warnings and admonishments about parties, boyfriends, drugs, drinking and anything else he could think could happen when giving as teenager a house for the weekend. He had been deliberately vague about their return time and insisted he would face time her each evening, 'just to be sure she was okay'. Emma had known better than to argue, nodding and agreeing as needed. And not saying anything when her mother had whispered in her ear as she hugged them goodbye, "we won't be back till after seven on Sunday. I promise".

Which meant they have another three hours before Peter needs to leave, another three erotic, sensual, illicit hours. But she knows he needs a rest and she wants to get closer emotionally. She wants to know more of the boy. She is still slightly mystified as to why she is so attracted to a boy who says so little about himself yet remembers everything she tells him; learns what she likes, what she doesn't like; is always ready to please her. And he wants to please her more than anything else, more than anyone else.

And yet their affair is still a secret. She tells Peter it's because it gives her more freedom to do things with him, 'no-one will know, so no-one can stop us'.

And he pretends to believe her because it suits him.

39

They talk for a while. About University, about what she wants to study and where she wants to travel. He asks her what she wants to see when she gets there and he answers her questions about the same subjects, tailoring his answers to line up with hers but making them just different enough to seem his own.

So logically the two of them should fit. But there's a gap, an area that they just don't talk about. And it's been a lingering doubt for long enough.

She wants to talk to him- or more accurately she wants him to talk to her about it- but it's really hard to ask the kind of question she needs to ask without running the risk of making things worse; of reminding him of a pain he might sooner forget. How can she raise the subject without making him close down and break away? So she stays silent, waiting and hoping that he will fill in the gaps for her. In his own time.

*

Peter knows he won't say anything. He's thought about it a lot, especially when they are apart. He, of all people, knows what her questions are going to be. He's living it. And it's not easy.

How do you tell someone why you have no friends? How do you explain what caused everyone at school to make you the butt of their jokes and that whatever the cause, everyone hates you anyway? How can you tell your lover that the only possibility you can think of is that it is just because of who you are, because of what you look like, how you speak, how you walk? Whatever it is, it must be your fault, because everyone else has friends, because no-one else is going through what you are facing. That means there is something dreadfully wrong with you and no matter how hard you've tried to change it, you're always going to be friendless. That means that there is no explanation for why this girl wants to be near you. Except that she will probably turn away eventually. So you have to hold on to her, have to do everything in our power to keep her. And that means not explaining that she is the only person in the world who likes you. No-one wants to be with anyone like that.

How can he tell her that he would do anything for her, whatever she asks, no matter how hard?

Except of course, he could explain.

He won't ever do that.

40

2001

The beeping stopped and the doors swished closed, changing the acoustics on the train and dimming the station announcers voice, half-sealing the passengers in a sound cocoon, where the unsettling noise of the pantograph above the carriage reverberated, making voices grow louder.

It would have been bearable but for the group of six women sitting at the far end of the carriage, sharing their own unique rendition of Dancing Queen with their captive audience. The man sitting nearby blinked wearily. For Matthew it had already been a long day. Starting with a morning meeting at seven a.m. and he'd been under pressure ever since. First for the financial analyses he'd promised to deliver immediately, and then a two-hour interrogation by HR about the trainee who had been dismissed the previous week. She was, he learned, taking the company to an industrial tribunal over the sexist attitudes and comments of her co-workers; attitudes that constituted sexual harassment, according to the letter from the lawyers. A letter that the HR business partner had waved repeatedly in his face when she was making her point. He'd had to sit through this, staying calm and responding in a dull monotone to all the accusations that had been made, denying everything. And he was pretty sure he hadn't made even half the comments she referred to. Well, maybe a bit more than half but even so.

The meeting had ended with his continued denial of the allegations- a strategy his line manager had told him was the only way to respond. Deny it all and then she'll accept the compromise agreement, because her lawyers will argue it's much less risky than having to try to prove the case in court. So he had toed the party line. Better for his career too, since an admission would have him publicly marked as a wimp AND a sexist. He'd be sacked and wouldn't find work easily again. So best stay schtum.

The only way to end a day like that had been with a few drinks. A small group of them had left early and gone to a wine bar some distance from the office. No-one wanted to be seen obviously celebrating having successfully 'repelled boarders'. Champagne at first was followed by bottles of Japanese beers and Matthew had left just as the shots started, shouts of 'lightweight' following him out of the door as he headed to his taxi. The short ride to Euston had got him there just in time to catch the penultimate train to his home town.

'Dancing Queen' morphed into 'I Will Survive'. The woman singing was no Gloria Gaynor but she was giving it the best she'd got and Matthew couldn't help but smile as she looked over, pointing directly at him as she told him that she had 'just walked in to find him here with that sad look upon your face'. He instinctively knew what was coming next. All six stood and shouted for him to 'go on now go, walk out that door,' six of them sweeping their arms across the carriage and pointing to the closed door.

At that moment the train began to move, sending the women off balance and causing them to fall onto the seats and onto one another in fits of shrieks and laughter. He smiled. At least they'll keep him awake, he thought, as the rocking motion of the train threatened its usual soporific effect.

Nineteen minutes later the train rolled into the station and he stood to leave, leaning against the side as he waited for the 'open' button to glow. One of the girls decided to have some fun with him and stumbled over to him, pulling his scarf away from his neck and sliding it around her body, teasing him to 'come and get it', a move that brought cheers and jeers from her friends.

On another day he would have responded and missed his station. But he needed to get home. So he told them his girlfriend was waiting for me. "So am I", shouted the girl. The train stopped and he pressed the button to open the door, prompting the girls to begin making clucking noises.

41

He could hear the cries of 'chicken' as he stepped down and out into the night, pulling his coat around him. He felt the night chill around his neck. Taking the stairs at the end of the platform, down to the passageway beneath the tracks, he crossed to the unattended and open gates.

His car was close to the entrance, about the only benefit of arriving early in the mornings. He pressed the button on the car door, opening it and sliding into the driver's seat. A push of a button to start the engine and then he turned on the heated seat and heated steering wheel. Without waiting for a perfectly clear screen, he reversed out of his space, hitting the brakes hard as soon as he heard a warning beeper sound. He looked behind him as a man walking back to his own car shouted out to him, telling him to watch where he was fucking going.

Matthew shook his head, put the car into gear and drove forward. He knew he shouldn't be driving but he also knew that the odds of him being caught by the police at this time of night were slim to none. He just had to make it along the main road, up into open countryside and he'd be almost home.

He turned left at the bridge and accelerated, lights on full beam as he left the town behind.

He thought the bright lights would be enough to see him safely home.

42

Emma washed her hands and put her coat on.

"I'm off now then," she said to no-one in particular. No-one replied and so she stepped through the kitchen door of the golf club and out into the car park. Checking her watch, she could see it was later than she had hoped. Nearly midnight. Which meant that her Mum and Dad would have gone to bed and she would have to walk home. She pulled the hood of her coat up and thrust her hands deep in her pockets as she started the short walk home. Though the Golf Club was out of the town, Emma lived a few hundred metres away in Hunter's Park. So it would only be around ten minutes before she was home, not even enough time to get her earphones out and listen to music. Turning right onto the main road that took her alongside the common, she settled into a steady pace, walking away from the club. It had been a pretty good night, she thought. She had learned the power of a smile and a gentle touch on arm or shoulder when she was taking and delivering orders. It hadn't taken her long to realise that the right style meant the tips were better. Have one for yourself had amounted to sixty-five pounds in drink tips this evening and she was getting close to the target that would enable her to buy a car. Or more accurately that would allow her to find a big enough deposit for her parents to contribute the rest and the insurance. Maybe another month and she'd be there.

Her eyes squinted shut as a car drove towards her, its headlights on full beam, dazzling her and forcing her to turn her head before it shot past and she could look down the road again, her night vision destroyed for a few moments. Fortunately, there weren't that many cars at this time. The trouble was that the most of those travelled at speed.

Slowly her vision returned and she moved back on to the hard asphalt, looking both ways before beginning to cross the road.

43

Matthew relaxed. He'd made it out of the town without being stopped. Which meant there was no more risk. He had never seen a police car stopping anyone out this way. Not even in the peak of summer, when visitors to the golf club stop off for a long liquid lunch at one of the country pubs nearby. Nor when rotund, brightly-dressed golfers left their club at night. Hardly a surprise, that. He'd bet that the local police big wig was probably a member. And no-one wants to ruin their career by taking down a senior officer now, do they?

He was getting desperate now. He should have gone on the train, he realised, and the need to pee was getting stronger. He pulled over to the side of the road and walked around the back of the car and stood by the side of the road, relieving himself of the last of his beers. He was only dimly aware of the noise of a growling engine closing rapidly, a glow of lights off to his left as he unzipped, a glow that grew swiftly brighter until it flung him into a spotlight, making his eyes wince at the brightness of the light, even as he turned away, to protect his eyes and his modesty. Then it was gone, the area immediately around him plunged into darkness as a cone of light disappeared into the night.

"Nice car," he muttered, zipping up and walking around the front of his car, climbing into the driver's seat and blinking at the instrument panel in front of him. Was it him or did the numbers look a little out of focus?

He clicked the seat belt into place and pressed his foot on the accelerator. Idly, he wondered if it had been a Ferrari or a Maserati- same engine so hard to tell. Ordinarily he might have raced after it, but there had been too much time and he certainly wouldn't catch it now. Still, no point hanging around. He might see a driver getting out of a stationery car and that would answer his question. His right foot pressed down and he took another look at the fuzzy dials, screwing up his eyes as he saw the needle move but not entirely sure if it was to 60 or 80 mph.

Whatever speed it was, the object that exploded on his windscreen, breaking the glass and bouncing up onto the roof shook him to his core. He had no memory of slamming on the brakes, of screaming "WHAT THE FUCK?!". He remembered coming to a screeching halt.

Adrenaline coursed through his body, obliterating the effects of alcohol in an instant. Shaking violently, he watched his hand reach out to the door handle and open the driver's door. His legs weren't strong enough to hold him as he climbed out of the car and looked back along the road, his hands gripping the car for support as he tried to focus on the thing in the road behind him. He heard the sound of the 'lights on' alert incessantly beeping and then a feral instinct kicked in and he closed the door hurriedly behind him, putting the roof light out and then taking a long look around him once he was less visible.

The faint flickering lights of a building were the only sign of life anywhere else. He stumbled back down the road, uncertain of what he would see, yet fearful of leaving evidence. He couldn't see much in the light from his taillamps, just a strange, dark shape off to the side of the road. Pulling out his phone, he clicked the torch on and looked down at the crumpled form in front of him and his heart skipped a beat.

Whatever it was now, it had once been a fully functioning human.

44

Panic-stricken, he ran back to his car, jumped in and pressed down on the accelerator. Yet the vehicle didn't move, the engine note rising loudly until he realised that he'd left the car in 'Park'. Seconds later he was feeding the car down the country lane, going as quickly as he could, praying there'd be no police in the area.

He made it back to his cottage without seeing anyone else. He slid the car inside the old wooden garage, parking the front of the car hard up against the far corner, trying to hide the damage as much as possible. He clambered out of the passenger side, staggered to his front door and stumbled inside, sliding to the floor in the darkness behind the closing door.

His heart was pounding now. He knew what he'd done. He knew what would happen. He'd murdered her and that wasn't going to end well. Fuck. Fuck. Fuck. And now he had left the scene of an accident without reporting it; a hit and run. Fuck. Why hadn't he phoned for the police, he asked himself, knowing that the answer was abundantly clear.

Then it hit him. What if she was still alive? Or had been still alive? What if he could have saved her? What if he still could? For a moment he contemplated making a 999 call and disguising his voice. But he knew that would just entrap him.

He closed his eyes and the sight of that mangled body appeared. The blood all over the head. The twisted limbs and that broken doll look of her head. No, she must have gone.

So the only thing to do was to get rid of the evidence that it was his car that had hit her. But how? The car windscreen was pitted and broken where the girl's body had hit. There would be blood in the glass, hair and skin fragments in the cracks, not to mention the stuff that would have attached to the 'A' pillar of the car. He'd read enough crime books to know about Lockhart's law- any contact leaves a trace- and whatever he did to clean it, there would always be some residual trace of her somewhere. No, he had to get rid of the car. Take it down the road and set fire to it. Surely that would destroy any traces.

At last, he had something he could do in response. Pushing down with both hands he began to stand up, trying to think what he had in the garage that might be flammable enough to torch the car properly. He'd find something to do the job with.

He pulled the front door open and then stopped abruptly. There was no point: Lockhart's law once again. Stuff from his colour of Mercedes would be embedded in her skull or fingernails or somewhere. Or there'd be a camera on a neighbour's house. Or in the golf club. And there would certainly be footage of him drunkenly leaving the station car park in a pristine car only a few minutes earlier. He'd be seen going to the car and driving off. He can't claim the car had been stolen.

His heart sank as he softly closed the front door. He was fucked. Resting his head against the door now, he stood still, trying to think what to do next, trying to find a solution, like a drowning man clutching for any kind of rope. He wanted to get another drink – maybe a drink would help him claim he wasn't drunk when driving; the alcohol in his system when they inevitably test him could have come from what he consumed at home. He didn't know how much alcohol was in him right now, but provided he looked to have drunk enough, and claimed it was recent, then he might be able to claim the excess alcohol was a function of home drinking. He stepped into the kitchen and poured himself a glass, knocking some straight back before rational thinking got in the way. He put the glass down in the sink and leant against the edge.

That's when reality hit him. There was no way out of this.

He was well and truly fucked.

45

Matthew pushed back from the sink and walked upstairs. He could at least take a shower and change before handing himself in. He turned the water on and took his shirt off, avoiding the sight of himself in the mirror, not wanting to face reality. And then he stopped. He'd seen the news conferences. Where people who had done something heinous and then gone off to clean up, where they were berated for being cold, callous, heartless psychopaths and narcissists. All adding to the tabloid fury and the likely length of their sentence.

He reached for his shirt. Then a new thought occurred to him. He should phone his solicitor friend Robin. Not long qualified but at least Robin knew something about the law. Maybe he would tell him what to do and what to say.

Matt went downstairs, made some coffee, and went into his lounge to make the call.

Robin answered on the sixth ring, his voice thick with sleep.

"Bloody hell Matt, what are you doing? It's well past midnight."

"Er yeah, I know mate and I'm sorry about that, but I need some advice."

Robin wasn't impressed.

"Unless you've killed someone, can't it wait till morning?"

"No, it can't wait."

"Why not?"

"Because I think I might have killed someone."

Robin' voice changed, sleep vanishing as he heard Matt's words.

"What do you mean you *might* have killed someone? It's hardly the kind of thing you don't notice, is it?"

"Well, I'm not absolutely certain but…"

Robin interrupted, his tone sharper still as his lawyer's brain kicked in:

"Firstly, are you formally asking me for legal advice?"

"Yes. I already said that."

"Good. In which case whatever you say to me is now confidential. Now what happened?"

Matthew described the accident.

"I did hit the woman, so how long a prison sentence am I going to have to serve?"

"Did you tell anyone you felt drunk?"

"No."

"And you weren't breath tested at any point?"

"No, I don't think anyone knows what's happened yet. Apart from you and me."

"And the girl of course. Look, go to bed now. Go off, have a shower, do your normal bed-time routine, and whatever you do, don't report anything to anyone. You need to do whatever you normally do. Call the insurance company about the car tomorrow."

Matthew took a deep breath. He couldn't understand how his friend was failing to get the whole point.

"Look Robin, much as I appreciate your advice, *I don't want to go to jail for murder*! And I don't want to have a ruined life just because of one small moment's distraction."

"Mate, you need to calm down. It's fine. I'll sort it out. I'll even keep you out of jail. And you'll probably only get a small fine."

"How?"

"Now *that* is what you pay me for. And I don't come cheap."

Matthew felt the relief roll over him.

"Get me off and it *will* be cheap," he said gratefully.

"Look," said Robin in a controlling tone, "what I am doing is because I've known you a long time. I'm bending the rules here and though you may not know it, you will owe me big time. I'll give you the script tomorrow. Understood?"

"I get it. And thanks."

46

Peter is waiting for a call. It is well past midnight and she should have phoned by now. She is normally so reliable he tells himself, more to prevent the tiny shred of jealousy and insecurity that is rising in the far corners of his mind than to confirm her pattern of behaviour, although it is true she's never not phoned when she said she would, from the first night they met. He checks his phone for the twentieth time. No message. No missed call. Once more he rings her, trying not to behave like the desperately insecure teenager who craves a response that he was rapidly becoming. Again. No answer.

He slides the phone under his pillow and closes his eyes. There's nothing he can do and he is sure she'll text or phone when she's ready. Won't she?

He drifts off into a fitful sleep, never far away from the lurking fear that something is wrong.

47

The early morning light is seeping through the curtains. It's not long after dawn and Pete has woken from a troubled sleep, filled with dreams of not being able to get back home, each time he turns a corner there's another road which leads to another and so on. He's glad to see he's still in his bed and reaches under his pillow for his phone.

Still nothing. No missed calls. No texts. Not even an email. He might as well get dressed and go out for a walk, he tells himself, knowing that inevitably he's going to go out and follow her route from work back to her house. Once he gets there it'll be late enough in the day for him to send a text and hope for a response. T-shirt and hoodie on top of jeans and he's ready, carefully stepping down the stairs to avoid waking his parents and then slipping on his trainers at the foot of the stairs and going out of the front door, turning the key in the lock as he pulls it shut gently.

His feet crunch along the driveway and soon he's on his way up the hill and turning onto the golf club road, scanning behind him for cars as he crosses over to the other side so that he faces traffic as he's always been taught to do. There's no sign of traffic this early, although he sees movement off to his left as he looks. It's a deer, bounding away through the trees and undergrowth; off, Peter assumes, to join the herd.

Several hundred metres farther on he jumps as a fox streaks across the road in front of him, obviously disturbed by his presence. Peter looks to where the fox has been and sees a small patch of dark shadow with a hint of red, just off from the side of the road, close to a large shrub. As he steps forward, his heart lurches. He knows what the red is.

Rushing forward he reaches the body on the ground and pushes aside the fabric of her jacket to see her face more clearly. He knows it is her. It's her jacket, her style, her presence. But the shape of her face is quite different. He can hardly bear to look at the side of her forehead that has been pushed in; a dark blue bruise visible across the swelling that has erupted all over that side of her face. The undamaged side is a blue-ish shade of grey and he gingerly reaches out to touch her, feeling a faint warmth as his fingers reach her face.

"Emma? Emma?" he calls, praying she will open her eyes and respond.

His prayers are unanswered. There's no response.

She must be dead.
But if she was killed on her way home last night, why isn't she cold?

48

His hands continue to trace the edges of her face, still trying to take in what might have happened. Then he sees it. The faintest movement of her chest. He turns his head to put his cheek close to her mouth and he can feel a damp warmth. She's barely breathing but it's there. His hands shake as he fumbles for his phone, calling for an ambulance in a tremulous voice, struggling to remember the name of the road, shouting down the phone, telling them to hurry up and get there. The telephone operator struggles to calm him enough to get him to carry out basic emergency checks.

"No, she's not conscious, she's been hit by a fucking lorry or something, what do you fucking think?"

"No, look I'm sorry, it's just…"

"I'll wait. Yes. Hang on, I'll check."

"Yes."

His emotions have taken over now. It's obvious she's almost dead. No-one can survive that kind of battering. This conversation is pointless. There's nothing more to be done and he doesn't want to answer any more stupid questions. His voice weakens as he faces the inevitable:

"She's breathing but only just."

"No, I can't see that much blood." Peter kneels once more, trying desperately to identify any kind of spontaneous movement. But he can see none. He leans close in, putting his face sideways by her soft, young, motionless lips, trying to sense an outflow of breath. But he knows. He doesn't need to do anymore because, instinctively, he has felt the life finally leave her body.

Struggling to breathe beneath the lung crushing weight of loss, he drops the phone and falls onto his side, his head inches from hers. His eyes fill, blurring his view of the lifeless eyes in front of him.

It is an eternity before he hears it. The sound of an emergency siren, fading in and out as the ambulance climbs and falls along the windy roads, the flashing blue light at first fleeting and intermittent then full and blinding, the dayglo vehicle barrelling down the road towards him. Peter stands and lifts his arms, enough of a signal for the vehicle to pull into the side of the road and for a young, bearded man to lean out of his window, reading the face of the youngster in front of him, knowing that this was indeed the place. His partner has climbed out of the vehicle and hurries over to the body. The paramedic kneels down beside her, asking Emma if she can hear him, talking calmly to her as he slips her hand on to the girls face and checks the carotid artery. But the man knows. He looks back at the driver, an almost imperceptible shake of the head transmitting the news and triggering his call back to base, explaining the situation.

Peter doesn't see the shake of the head, nor does he register the words the driver is speaking into his handset.

Peter doesn't know that he will never be able to talk to her again.

49

The old-fashioned alarm clock shatters the silence with a loud ringing bell. Matthew's heart skips a beat in shock, even though he had already been awake for some time, staring at the slowly brightening ceiling above his bed. He has relived a different, flatter kind of sound a hundred times throughout the night; the sound of the person hitting his windscreen; he's seen the sight of a fleeting dark shape bouncing across his view, the image of a broken, twisted body lying on the edge of the road appearing, unbidden, haunting him as he tries to stop it returning.

It's no use. He'll have to get up. Once out of bed, he goes to the bathroom and turns the shower on, steam forming over the mirror as he urinates then flushes the toilet, glad not to have to see his own face as he steps under the hot stream, opening his mouth as he stands still, trying to breathe beneath the deluge of water running down his face, focussing on the feeling. It's not working. He takes a large dollop of shower gel and vigorously washes his hair and face, rubbing hard but failing to dislodge the invisible and indelible particles of shame and guilt.

Twenty minutes later he is standing in his kitchen, a mug of coffee in hand as he looks out. Can it really only be 12 hours since he was sitting happily drinking a beer with his colleagues? His phone rings. It's his lawyer.

"Hi Matthew, how are you doing?"

"Not so good. I don't want to mess you about, but I think I should just go and tell the truth."

"Don't be stupid."

"Look, I know it'll have consequences, but I did hit her."

"All you actually know is that you hit something."

"Robin, I saw the clothing. It was a woman."

"There is absolutely nothing you can do to change things now. If it is a person, then they will already have been found and you won't gain from putting your head up. If she's dead, that cannot be reversed, can it?"

"No but..."

"So the choice now comes down to what consequences you want for you."

"Well, I really should..."

"No," interrupted Robin firmly. "Take my advice: Guilt is for Catholics. For a start you don't actually know if she is dead."

"I'm pretty sure."

"Even so. You have no idea what caused the death."

"Duh, my car?"

"No. You don't know that she hadn't had a brain haemorrhage or an aneurysm or a heart attack… she may have fainted and fallen into the path of the car. You can never know for sure what precipitated the incident. It'll be impossible to tell if her body has been badly damaged subsequently. So you won't know for sure that you were the actual cause of death."

"Well, maybe not. Oh Fuck, I don't know. It's pretty obvious and certain though, isn't it?"

"Maybe, but nothing is absolutely certain here."

"What do I do then? How do I explain not stopping to help her? How do I explain leaving her to die, for fuck's sake?"

"You don't."

50

"What do I say then?" asks Matthew.

"You tell them that you think you hit a deer. No, better yet, tell them you were absolutely certain you hit a deer. It will explain why you didn't report the accident and explain the damage to your car. You must also say that you didn't get out of the car to look. You stopped briefly, composed yourself and then continued home, certain, as you were, that it had been a deer."

Matthew swallowed, imagining having to say those words, knowing they were lies.

"The worst that can happen is that you can be charged with driving without due care and attention. They can't say you were driving dangerously because there will be no evidence to that effect. It's the same as if you reversed into a tree. Not paying proper attention but no more than that. And since killing a deer does not require to be reported to anybody, it is not unreasonable to argue that you had no inkling it had been a person. I mean who would be walking around those roads at night without a torch anyway?"

"So what will I be looking at if I'm convicted?"

"Oh, you'll be convicted. Especially if you don't want to make things worse. Plead guilty. It is a summary offence. No jail because there is no option to place you in custody."

"Really?"

"It's a known issue. There is a huge gap in sentencing which they'll deal with in time but for now, you won't even be banned from driving. A few penalty points and a sizeable fine and you'll be done."

"Are you sure? Sounds too good to be true."

"I'm sure. If you had been drinking and driving, then it would be a very different story but there is no evidence that you were over the limit at the time of the offence. So it all depends on you remembering what happened- i.e. you hit a deer and didn't look- and then holding that line. I mean, it was hardly deliberate, was it?"

Matthew still wasn't concentrating on what his solicitor was saying.

"Christ this is a fucking mess. Why was she there at that time of night?"

"Look Matthew. Pay attention Was knocking her over a deliberate act?"

"No, of course it bloody wasn't."

"So there you are. Wait till there is some publicity and then tell me. I'll call the law on your behalf."

"Okay. I still don't know how I'm going to live with myself though."

Even Matthew was surprised by the chill in Robin's reply:

"That, my friend, is your problem and yours alone. But I know you will find a way."

The line went dead and Matt stared blankly at the screen of his phone. It felt as if he was not really here, as if he was a million miles away just looking in on a life that wasn't his anymore. The picture faded and he remained standing, waiting for the world to turn once more, waiting for something to take him away from all this.

His reverie was broken by the sound of a loud thumping on front the door. What the fuck? The police had obviously found him already. No time to phone Robin back. Perhaps, he thought, perhaps it was for the best; a kind of swift justice. He sniffed, brushed his hands up his face and through his still wet hair. If it was to be now at least he was relieved.

The banging started up once more.

"Alright, I'm coming," he called out before unlocking and then lifting the latch on the front door.

51

It wasn't the police. It was his neighbour, John.

"I want a word with you."

"Why? What for?"

"Because of all the bloody racket you made last night."

"Eh?"

"You come back, revving your fucking car engine, banging the garage doors, not to mention slamming the front door. Have you no consideration for other people?"

"Look, John, I'm really sorry about that. I was probably a bit pissed..."

That was when his brain began to work again and an instinct for self-preservation kicked in.

"I was probably pissed off at some work things. You know how it is, you think about things after the event and sometimes you can forget to be quiet. I'm sorry that I was noisy."

"Yeah well, I just wish you'd thought about it last night."

"I'm sorry, I really am. I'll be more careful next time."

"Alright, be sure you do. Anyhow, I was surprised to find you in to be honest. Aren't you going off to work today?"

"Ah no, day off. Something we all need occasionally, eh?

John didn't answer immediately. He was already on his way back to his own front door.

"Alright for you," he said. "I've got to go to work, even if I did have a broken night's sleep," he added over his shoulder.

Matthew shut his door and went in to phone the office. He would tell them he had a family emergency and couldn't come in today. If he was lucky, his boss would be in the morning meeting and wouldn't take the call.

Much easier to leave a voicemail.

52

Peter was sitting on his bed, the local paper spread out in front of him. There were two pages of pictures and commentary on the accident. Pictures of the road, the police tape strung out and used to seal off the area,

Most importantly there was a picture of the man involved. A wanky-looking banker. It was taken with a telephoto lens and showed him coming out of a front door, dressed for work. The house was somewhere along a country lane that ran out past the common and the golf club. It looked vaguely familiar. And though there was no number on the door, it wouldn't take long to find the place, just by walking along the road. He wanted to go there now. Go and tell him just what he had done to Emma and her dreams. And what he done to destroy the future that Pete and Emma had planned.

It wasn't fair. It wasn't right that a man should mow down an innocent girl coming home after working in the community, should break 29 bones in her body, fracture her skull, smash her jaw and yet simply walk away, paying a fine. Was that the value that you put on a life? A few hundred pounds? That fine was worth less than the price of her weight in venison. Her lifeless body was worth less than a fucking deer's? How can that be allowed to happen?

Peter knows that he can't bring her back but there should be a price to pay for this heinous act that today leaves the perpetrator, the murderer, free to roam the streets, free to have a life, free to move on with none of the loss, none of the unbearable burden that Emma's loved ones had to bear.

Perhaps, thought Peter, it was time to pay a visit to the moron. Let him know how it felt to die too, perhaps.

He read through the rest of the paper, finally seeing a full paragraph about Emma. Her school record, some quotes from her parents at the inquest and a response to the news that the wanker had only been charged with careless driving. Careless fucking driving.

Peter was sure he could find the man's home easily.

There was a soft knock on his door, and his mother put her head in the room.

"I'm just checking to see how you're doing?" she said, the Australian-style upward inflection at the end adding the question mark.

"If only I could have done something to help her. I was there for fifteen minutes before the ambulance arrived and I didn't know what to do."

"There really wasn't anything you could have done. She was so badly hurt by the time you got there that all you could have done would not have saved her. The damage was too great and you did your best."

"But if I had known…"

"Look Peter, you have to understand this. There was nothing more you could have done. You found her when she could have been out there for hours more before if you hadn't looked. And then you called an ambulance. No one could ask any more of you."

"But all they did was see if she was dead. Nobody did anything to actually save her."

"That's because she had already gone. Pete. You know that."

His shoulder slumped and his eyes filled as he recognised the truth of her arguments and was forced to acknowledge his impotence, both now and then.

"It's just that… it's just that…"

Pete's mother reached out to him, sitting down on the bed and putting her arm around his shoulder; that simple action set off the emotional turmoil that had been barely contained. He shuddered as the tears came.

53

Matthew was sitting in bed on Sunday morning, the national and local papers spread out in front of him. The local gazette had moved the story of the inquest and Matthew's conviction to a small legal paragraph on page 5. He was grateful for this because the more newsworthy pictures of a funeral and grieving family had been on the front page only a few weeks ago.

His phone rang. It was Robin.

"Hello mate. Things good?"

"Kind of."

"Kind of? I thought you'd be dead chuffed."

"Well, I am but I still feel a bit awkward. Someone pointed me out the other day and I know it's because of the accident. I heard them say I must have been drunk to hit her. I'm pretty sure I wasn't too far over the limit, if at all frankly, but I couldn't say that could I? Honestly, I just wish I had seen her. and this need never have happened."

"You were unlucky Matt. Just bloody unlucky."

"I know. I wish she had been wearing brighter clothing or at least carrying a torch, just something that would have made her stand out better. And why was she crossing the road anyway? Right in front of me?"

"Just your bad luck mate. And next time stay off the drink."

"At least I was fortunate enough to have you in my corner anyway. It was your advice that has kept me out of jail. Even if the police had worked out what might have happened, you know from the way the body fell etc, without your guidance I'd have given myself up."

"All I can say is that I am glad you didn't. And you're right, I am a pretty amazing lawyer, aren't I?

"I know, I know, it's hard to be humble when you've all that talent," laughed Matthew. "How's life treating you anyway? Who's your girlfriend this week?"

"Ah, well I wanted to talk to you about that. "

"Eh?"

"I have just met this gorgeous girl and, importantly, she has friends. Nice friends. Fancy joining us all for brunch on Sunday?"

Matt knew there was more to this than Robin was letting on, but he knew too that he needed to get out soon, just for his own sanity, if nothing else.

"Okay mate. Sunday it is."

"Cool. I'll send you the details."

54

This is the place. Pete checked the photo once more but he knew it wasn't necessary. The image of that front door was indelibly engraved in his mind. The light was fading fast now and he had time to check he wasn't being observed as he stood by the driveway, trying to look nonchalant as he pretended to be lost. There was no one in sight. Opposite the house were fields and forest and on his side of the road all the houses were set well back from the road, straggling trees and shrubbery to the front of each one. There was a sizeable hedge separating this house from the neighbouring property and no lights were on in either one.

He strode up to the front door and banged the door knocker loudly. Too loudly. He shrank inside his clothing in reaction, not wanting to draw unnecessary attention to himself.

He waited.

No response.

Another loud knock.

Still no response, so he walked around the front to the garage standing to the side of the property. The doors were made up of a series of folding panels, each one wooden with a run of dusty square glass panels above, through which Peter squinted. Too dark to see. He pulled his small metal torch from the side pocket of his backpack and shone it inside, the beam picking out a long wooden bench at the back, above which an empty pinboard was fixed. There was little else to see, except for several boxes pushed under the bench and to the side of the garage. There was no car. He looked at the doors and was pretty sure he could open the lock but there was nowhere in the garage to hide. He turned away, deciding he'd do better to stick to his original plan. He did a quick check to see no-one was watching and then climbed over the mid-height fencing that ran from the front corner of the house to the hedgerow separating this property from the old folks home next door. Soon he was settled in beneath the fence and foliage, backpack pushed to his side, and tucked well out of sight from anyone who might peer across from either property.

A minute later he sighed in frustration. He needed to pee. He crawled out and stood close to the hedge running the length of the side of the garden. There was only one window overlooking this patch of land, and it looked like a bathroom window to judge from the frosted glass. He unzipped and relaxed. He was almost finished when he heard the sound of a powerful car sweeping up the lane towards this end of the village. Hurriedly he zipped up and scuttled back into his original place, breaking some twigs in his haste, hoping that the damage wouldn't be seen by anyone before he had accomplished what he set out to do.

He was back just in time as bright lights swept across the front of the house and stopped facing the fence. Peter moved deeper into the hedgerow, crouching and pushing in backwards, using the backpack to protect him as he settled deeper and deeper in. He heard the door of a car opening, music coming from inside mixing with the chime of a warning alert followed by a creaking and groaning of wood. He heard the wheels of the garage door moving on metal and then a bang. Peter waited until the man returned to move the car into the garage then shifted the backpack round to his front and tried to control his breathing. The car engine cut out and the noise of a car door shutting and the garage closing reached his ears. Moments later the front door slammed and a light went on.

Unzipping his backpack, he pulled out three plastic containers that once held milk and placed them on the ground in front of him. He would wait until it was fully dark. He didn't want to be seen running away once he'd started.

55

Inside the house, the driver walked into the kitchen, opened the freezer, pulled out a bottle of vodka and poured a shot. The first one wasn't enough. He poured a second, knocked it back and replaced the bottle in the freezer. He glanced out of the kitchen window, noting the darkening sky and then moved away, hesitating as he reached the doorway. He wanted another shot but knew it wouldn't be just one. Sighing, he flicked off the light and went into the lounge.

Outside, Peter couldn't sit still. He knew waiting would be the better course of action but he had to look now. He pulled himself forward and slowly stood up, looking around and then ducking down as he ran over to the nearest window. After a short pause, he stretched up to take a quick look.

It was the kitchen window. He couldn't see anyone but there was a light on in the room beyond the kitchen. Someone was definitely there; there was a shifting change in the light, a shadow moving marginally, and he ducked back down below the sill.

He wished he'd thought about this a bit more. What had seemed like a straightforward plan was a lot more difficult in person. And the simple physics were not on his side. You can't really use plastic for a Molotov cocktail and there was nothing flammable on the outside of the house. He'd need to get in and pour the petrol in. And that would be risky. Maybe he could smash a window. But the shadowy figure inside might hear it.

And most importantly, he needed to be sure he could be well away quickly. Once he was in the woods, he'd be fine. He'd been in and around this for all of his youth and could find his way round even in the dark. But the surroundings of the house, especially at the back, were not familiar.

So perhaps his best bet was to see if he could set the fire at the very back of the house. He crept round to the far side of the house to check out his options.

There was a broken air vent he could probably pour it through, but petrol is quite pungent. He'd need to be quick. Even so, he worried that the way that vent was positioned it meant half the stuff probably wouldn't make it through to the inside. Plus it might splash back onto his clothing. Shit. He didn't want to go home reeking of petrol. Or burnt.

Maybe the window? The windows were large leaded lights. Perfect. He could push in a pane of glass and then pour the fuel in quickly. He dropped down and took the top off the large milk carton that was full of unleaded siphoned from his father's car.

A bright light came on in the room behind the window.

Fuck.

He stepped to the side, replacing the lid on the bottle, and waited while whoever was there moved over to the door and drew a set of curtains. Then he heard it. The sound of a woman's voice.

"Hey gorgeous, what are you up to?"

Fuck.

He hadn't heard a car draw up. He'd been so intent on his task that he'd lost all connection to his surroundings.

Fuck.

This wouldn't work now. The risks had doubled. And it was the man he was targeting not the girl.

He needed to go to his back-up plan.

56

He picked up the carton and headed round to the side of the property, clambering back over the fence panel and pushing himself up against the garage side wall.

This would be better in some ways. The man might keep his house intact but there would be at least a sense of poetic justice from the removal of the weapon that was used on Emma. And it would mean he hadn't just let the crime go completely unpunished.

Peter unscrewed the top of the carton and poured the contents liberally over the back corner of the garage, leaving a line of fuel to run along the side. A quick glance at the house and then he moved closer to the driveway, pulled out a box of matches and held one on the side of the box, one finger on the end of the match, the head of the match on the striking plate. He flicked the match and sent it towards the garage, where it dropped and went out.

Shit.

The next one flew a little farther. A loud whoosh accompanied the sight of petrol lighting explosively and spreading along the wall to the back.

Peter turned and sprinted as fast as he could for the roadway and for the trees beyond. As he crossed the road he saw a set of headlamps headlong in his direction, full beam on. He closed his eyes and crashed into the hedgerow, holding his arm in front of him. His legs pounded through the undergrowth and emerged onto grass on the far side. His head went down and he ran as hard as he could across the grass and up towards farm buildings in the distance. He turned as he reached a copse and let his back rest against a tree trunk. Behind him a new source of light had risen.

He breathed a sigh of relief as the aftermath of adrenaline kicking in and draining him of energy. And yet he couldn't rest now. He had to dispose of the bottles and make it home without being seen before the last stroll up the road and into the driveway of his home.

He pushed himself up from the tree and started the walk home, a journey that would probably take about an hour. Soon the light source had vanished and his eyes became accustomed to the darkness and the sounds of the forest. He felt his pulse rate slowing down now, the peace and tranquillity of the night air and open landscape calming him as the stress and fear faded. He began to think about what he'd say when he got home, how he'd try to find out what had finally happened at the garage without being too obvious.

An hour later his father was standing in the front room as he saw a very weary son turn into the driveway. He paused and smiled as Pete looked up and lifted a hand in a half-hearted acknowledgement without stopping his trudge to the door. Once inside, he went straight upstairs to his room.

Peter's father looked over at the door of the front room, wishing his son had come in to see him; wishing he knew what to say to help comfort him; wishing the accident had never happened. But he knew time would heal eventually. What mattered now was just giving the boy space to adjust.

Upstairs, Peter lay down on his bed and looked at the photo in his hand. It was the last one they had taken together. A selfie, her smile radiant as they both looked directly into the lens, the magical sparkle in her eyes perfectly captured. The photo was worn, the edges frayed, the texture softening. He was losing the only tangible connection he had left. He wanted to know when; when he would be able to look at it without that crushing pain in his heart. And when it did, he would have lost her forever. That was what hurt the most.

Downstairs, his father saw the blue flashing lights in the distance.

Best not to ask.

57

The offices were not palatial. 'Unvarnished' was the name of the organisation and the description was more than accurate for the basic facilities here.

"What do you think?'

"Of what?"

Darren was pitching his latest lead to James, the editor.

"The idea."

James looked into the camera lens and grimaced.

"I don't know. It's a bit low-level, isn't it?"

"Might be a good line though. It's the kind of thing that gets picked up and we could use some more views. Surely it's worth a phone call to the guy, isn't it?"

"Maybe. Look," he added, pushing his fingers through his thick hair, "talk to the kid and see what he says. Then we can decide. And make sure every word is recorded."

"Er yeah, I know boss, it was the kit that didn't work last time, remember, not me."

"Yeah, yeah. They always say that. Blame it on the tech. Not this time though."

"Okay."

James was the new-found editor of a publication called 'Unvarnished', a local newspaper that was building a reputation as the place to go if you wanted to leak salacious details of an affair, dob in a prominent politician or have a go at corruption. It was founded after one big story, an exposé of a local MP's clandestine dealings with companies bidding for large and lucrative government contracts. The MP had died suspiciously close to the court case that would have exposed the full details of the entire affair. Though nothing had been proven, there was little doubt that his unexpected heart attack while alone in his car had raised a number of concerns. There had been an autopsy that was equivocal in nature and the inquest had returned an open verdict. But the story had been enough to secure a decent level of sales.

And although, logically, the newspaper's primary focus was the moral high ground, it wasn't averse to picking up stories that were less well sourced than the national and mainstream media. Always careful to ensure that items were seen as 'opinion' rather than fact and the text was usually littered with exclusions and legal get-outs, in case the material was less than accurate.

There had been a few close shaves in the early days and now they relied upon 'opinion' contributors, allowing for a leeway that fact-based reporting wouldn't provide. Even so, the laws of defamation still exist and the well-being of the paper was perpetually under threat. Hence the discussion.

"So what else have we got?"

"Not much for today. I was going to write about the mayor with the penchant for powder, but we can't get any pictures. Everyone knows he loves it but without the photo we have nothing. No-one is prepared to say that they saw him or supplied it. And after last month's episode with the undercover officer who wasn't... I mean how was I supposed to know he was a fucking psycho?"

"I would have thought it would have been obvious."

"Yeah well, he was pretty convincing boss. And he did a good line in why no-one had heard of him."

"Yeah, I know, Darren. Look, go with the kid for now. And try to be sympathetic, you know? Give him room, plenty of line and then reel it in, whatever he's got to say."

58

"Hi. Peter?"

"Yeah."

"It's Darren, from 'Unvarnished'."

"Oh yeah. Hi."

"Is now a good time to talk?"

"Hang on a moment."

The phone went dead for a few moments.

When the voice returned, the nervous edge had left Peter's attitude.

"Sorry about that. Just wanted to shut the door so we could be sure to have some privacy."

Automatically, Darren nodded.

"Okay, so what did you want to talk about."

"It's just that there's something I thought you might be interested in. Especially since the police aren't really focussed at the moment."

"I'm not sure when they *are* focussed to be honest with you, except when they don't like us, that is. But still...look Peter, I know it might be a bit of a difficult time for you, but do you mind if I record this?"

"I don't know."

"It just saves us misquoting you. Actually, it might just be better if you come in. We need to have a face-to-face discussion anyway, especially when we are picking up new material, so can you come in and see us?"

"Er yeah, okay then. This afternoon okay?"

Three hours later, Darren looked at the young man in front of him. This was his first glimpse of the boy whose girlfriend had been run over and he was surprised by the coldness that he saw. He hadn't expected wailing grief but there was a remoteness, a distance in the lad's demeanour that was slightly unnerving. He had a pale face, his hair was long, not overly so but a deliberate style, not in-keeping with most razor-styles today, and there was no sign of any facial hair. Yet the voice was deeper than you would expect, if you were matching voices to faces. Often the way though, thought Darren. On the other hand, the black hoodie he was wearing was no surprise.

"Peter, let me first start by saying how sorry I was to read about what happened to Emma. It was a tragic loss and you have my sympathy."

Darren didn't expect the reply he got:

"It wasn't a tragic loss."

"What do you mean?" asked the reporter.

"She was murdered by an animal in a car. It wasn't just tragic. It was a criminal act."

"Please accept my sympathies even so."

"No, you misunderstand me. Those words were not mine."

Darren was confused now, unable to stop himself frowning.

"So whose were they?" he asked.

"Emma's father's."

"Well, I get that. It's easy to understand why he might say that."

Peter paused and looked down briefly, before raising his cold eyes and replying:

"It's what else he had to say that you need to hear."

59

Darren sat forward: "Go on then, tell me."

"Emma's Dad said he wanted the man responsible for the death to burn in hell. And that it couldn't come soon enough, as far as he was concerned."

"Go on."

"Well, it's obvious, isn't it?"

"I'm sorry, what do you mean?"

"He wanted the man to burn. Then the house is torched. 2+2."

Darren, pursed his lips as he digested what he was hearing. 'Grief stricken father torches daughter's killer' would make a good headline, even if the killer wasn't there at the time.

"When did he tell you this?"

"At the funeral. He came over to me and told me she'd be avenged."

"Do you have anything to back this up?"

"What, like a film?", sneered Peter.

"Okay, fair enough. I just don't know if there's much we can do with this."

"I told the police but they just ignored it. Didn't even write it down. But he shouldn't get away with it. The way I see it, if he gets off, he's no better than the driver. People should pay for their actions."

"Well, I don't know what we can do, but let me run this by my boss and we'll see if we have enough for a piece. If not, well…"

"If not, you might at least have some contacts who would help?"

There was a long exhalation of breath while Darren thought about it and then a decision:

"Okay, leave it with me and I'll let you know if we're going to run anything."

Darren's instincts were twitching. Maybe there was a bit of backstory he could use here? Play it up. Make the girl a saint and the loss even more tragic? More motive for justified revenge? Could he trust the boy? Did it matter? A question to check, maybe.

"Who else could it have been?"

"I don't know. All I do know is that losing a wonderful daughter is reason enough to take revenge, isn't it?"

"Maybe. Look, leave it with me. I'll let you know."

So that was it. The interview. Nothing very much there in reality. Maybe they could beef up the motive for the arson? He'll talk to James.

He put his notes back down on his desk, just as a new thought registered in his mind.

It had been fleeting; barely a nanosecond. Other people probably wouldn't have noticed but Darren's journalistic instincts had picked it up. A twitch at the corners of Pete's mouth. Not a smile. Not a joy. More a hint of satisfaction. Or something else? He couldn't quite put his finger on it but there was something there.

He shrugged. Who knows what it was. Maybe the kid just wants justice to prevail.

Now that would be novel.

60

"You can't."

"I have to."

"No, you don't. You don't have to do anything."

Peter threw a book clean across his bedroom and collapsed onto the bed.

His father was standing by the door, breathing deeply as he tried to control his frustration. He'd known that Peter had been up to no good and it hadn't been difficult to put things together; the anxious looks whenever he heard a siren, repeated visits to the front window all told a story.

His parents had already talked about what they thought had happened and why. They had disagreed on what to do about it though. His father was all for owning up and pleading that the poor boy was just grief stricken. His mother was much more practical. Stay quiet. No need to tell anyone. Insurance would cover the costs of the damage. No-one was hurt. Pete would know he'd been lucky.

Until, that was, the news that Emma's father had been arrested for the arson attack on the driver's home. He had been seen walking along the village road a number of times, had recently filled a petrol can which- despite his claim of needing it for a lawnmower- was proof of preparation. And an eye-witness had seen someone wearing the same kind of clothing as the man getting into a car only a few minutes after the fire was reported. Neighbours confirmed the man had returned home some twenty minutes after the fire had started, fire investigators confirmed the accelerant that had been used. And of course, there was no need to look for a motive.

Now it lent even more weight to Pete's father's argument that he should go to the Police and confess.

"But how will you live with yourself if Emma's Dad is found guilty for a crime that you committed?"

"Dad, it's simple. If I had been luckier the driver would have lost more than his car and garage. As it is, they'll let Emma's Dad go eventually and I won't be arrested."

"You might be right but it's a cruel attitude, isn't it?

"No crueller than having your girlfriend killed."

"But what about Emma's Dad? It's hardly fair, is it?"

"Oh, he'll be fine. Like I say, they'll never prove it anyway."

The sound of footsteps coming up the stairs caused them both to stop speaking while they waited. The steps came nearer and Pete's father moved away from the door as his mother appeared and gave Pete a clear instruction:

"Don't you dare say a thing, Pete."

"I wasn't going to."

"Look," said his mother, "Emma's Dad has only got retirement to look forward to. You have got a whole life to build. You want to go to university, don't you?"

She didn't wait for an answer.

"I tell you this much, one thing is guaranteed."

61

Peter and his father both looked directly at his mother, waiting for her to explain.

"If you admit arson then you'll never be free. Arson is a life sentence."

'I don't think you get a life sentence for arson, Mum."

"You do. Just not in jail."

"Eh?"

"No university is going to take you if you've a criminal record for arson. If Emma's dad is innocent, then he won't be charged and if he is charged, then he won't be found guilty, assuming the courts do their jobs properly."

Peter's father recoiled as he heard those words, his face turning to look directly at her, frowning as he responded:

"What do you mean if he is innocent? We know what he did!"

"Yes, but we don't know what else her dad might have already done or might have planned. For all we know he would have set fire to the house with them both in it. So you can argue that Pete might have saved their lives by torching the garage."

Pete couldn't hold back any longer:

"I wish I *had* torched the house properly."

"Pete, you don't mean that."

"I do. The man that killed her didn't give a shit and nor do I."

Now it was Peter's father's turn to join in:

"You don't know that. You don't know how he feels. It was all a dreadful accident and sooner or later you'll have to make peace with that."

"No Dad, that's not true. His ridiculous story of a deer doesn't make sense. He must have known it was her. And he shouldn't have been driving anyway. He was bound to hit someone eventually."

Peter's father was reluctant to concede the point.

"Well, that's not how the court saw it."

"However the court saw it," said his mother, "you're all going to keep quiet. No one is going to tell anyone anything. What would be the point of incriminating this family for something that caused no-one any real harm? Maybe if someone had been hurt it would be different, but it was only a crappy old garage that burned down."

"Okay," said Peter's father. "I'll leave it."

"Peter?"

"*I'm* not likely to say anything, am I Mum?"

"Good. That's settled then. Now I want you both downstairs for dinner. It's time we got some semblance of normality back in this family."

'It'll take more than dinner', thought Peter's father, wisely holding back from expressing that view.

62

Present Day

"I'm going to go."

"Don't waste your time."

Robinson's face shows his frustration.

"Joanne, it's only a waste of time if I don't go. And anyway, I want some answers. You told me not to chase the doctor, so what's left? There must be something they can tell us by now. We have more CCTV cameras than any other country on earth so how can they not have found the car? How can they not have found the driver?"

"It's up to you." she says flatly.

"Thanks for your support."

She lights another cigarette and turns back to stare out of the window once more, looking in the direction of the front garden and the street where Chloe died, her eyes glazing over almost immediately. Robinson knows the conversation, if that's what you can call it, is over.

Resigned, he leaves the house, closing the front door softly and climbing into the family car for the drive into town. He drives around the back of the police station and parks up, ignoring the 'reserved for police only' sign screwed to the wall in front of him. He walks to the front of the building and into the waiting area. There are thick glass panels above a counter, separating the waiting room and a small reception area, behind which a door leads into the offices. To the side of the screens is an electronically controlled door with a security code lock above the handle.

He presses the very obvious bell on the counter and waits. He presses again and waits once more. It's a good job it's not an emergency, he mutters, pressing for a third time, holding his finger on the bell for long enough to irritate. Still no reply. He resists the temptation to bang on the glass, turning to the three wooden chairs ranged against the wall and sitting down while he thinks about what to do next.

The front door swings open and a well-built plain clothes officer wearing a large hoodie and low-slung jeans goes over to the door and begins keying in the code.

"Excuse me, I'd like to speak to someone about my daughter's murder."

The man turns slowly and looks over at Robinson.

"What murder?"

"My daughter's. It's been all over the media for Christ's sake, how come you don't know?"

"Ah," says the man, "I recognise you now. I'm sorry but we're not treating it as a murder. It's a hit and run, even though she was tragically killed in the accident."

"For fuck's sake."

"Don't take that tone with me."

"It was a murder. There's no way it was an accident."

"That's not what the officer investigating says, and his voice is the one that matters."

"It isn't."

"I think you'll find it is. Now if there's nothing else…".

"What I mean is my daughter's is the voice that matters and she's. not here to be heard. So I'm speaking for her."

The officer can tell this is going to be a tricky one.

"Alright. If you're going to be difficult just wait here. and I'll get D.I. Winslaw,"

63

Moments later it's clear that DI Winslaw isn't in the building.

Robinson tries a different tack.

"Look, I know it's not your case but can you give me some advice then?"

"I really haven't…"

Robinson is getting frustrated now.

"I'm sorry but I think there was a reason she was run over, and I want to find out what that was."

The officer relents slightly.

"That's understandable."

"And the man who seems to have something to do with it is one of my neighbours."

Now the officer looks more interested.

"You think he killed the girl?"

"No. At least not directly."

"So what are you saying then?"

"I just want to know if there are, say, any reasons I should be careful, if you know what I mean."

"Look. I can't give out any information about people who may or may not be in our records. Whoever it is." He frowns and then asks the question anyway.

"Who is it?"

"Dr Samza."

The officer relaxes and his shoulders soften.

"You're joking, aren't you? Why on earth would he be involved? He's a great bloke- been a force doctor for years. Even helps us personally when he's here for a prisoner. Helped sort my physio problem out a treat, he did, and I didn't even have to go to the surgery. Got the prescription I needed on the spot."

The man puts a hand on the base of his neck and begins to roll his shoulder round by way of proof.

"The doctor will have nothing to do with this, I can assure you of that. Now if you don't mind, I really must get organised."

Robinson watches as the man disappears pulling the door shut behind him.

'So that is that', thinks Robinson. The man is a saint as far as the police are concerned. But he isn't convinced. A reputation for ad hoc consultations doesn't mean a thing. Whatever is going on, it's clear he'll get no help from law enforcement if he wants to find out the truth about Samza. He can't just let the matter drop. He owes it to Chloe and, even though Joanne doesn't seem to want to know right now, one thing is certain; she needs to know what happened.

They both deserve to learn the truth. And no-one wants to help.

So he'll just have to find out the truth for the both of them.

64

Robinson sits back in his chair and looks at his notes. He's been researching for an hour and found out very little. The doctor doesn't have a big online presence and has a very limited profile on the health service website. He's registered with the GMC, did a medical degree in Newcastle, works at the local practice, makes himself available for private consultations. He published a paper a number of years ago on the interaction of various stimulant and depressant drugs, most of which was way beyond Robinson's understanding and has spoken at some drug company conferences. That is pretty much all the information he can uncover.

There's an old photo of Samza that looks vaguely familiar, in the way that any fuzzy photograph is reminiscent of a time and place.

Otherwise, it's all pretty consistent with someone who doesn't want to be visible. Perhaps that's significant in itself. Who, but people who have things to hide, is quite so invisible online nowadays?

Even so, it doesn't help any to know that.

He's going to have to find another way to find out what's really going on.

65

The sky is slowly lightening in the East, thinning the darkness beyond the curtains and replacing it with a grey wash now visible at the edges of the fabric. Joanne has barely slept once the anaesthetising effects of a steady stream of vodka through the evening have worn off, leaving her exhausted and anxious, awake but barely functioning, her eyes red and sore. She yawns and looks across at her sleeping husband. For a moment she is seized with the urge to kick him into wakefulness, to ask him how he can just sleep through this nightmare, wanting to make him suffer in the same way as she is suffering. But waking him, depriving him of sleep won't accomplish that. Aside from the likely argument that will result, it won't solve anything. It won't make her less fatigued and it certainly won't ease her pain. She can't help being deliberately clumsy as she pushes back the duvet and slips her legs out of the bed. Facing away from her husband, she allows her legs to swing to the floor and help her sit up and then pushes herself off the bed, giving an extra hard push as she rises. Still there is no change in the heavy breathing to her right. She goes to the bathroom, pees and washes her hands in the gloom, slurping up water in the palm of her hands to quench the thirst and then makes her way down the stairs, leaning a little too heavily on the wall as she goes down the stairs. Her head is pounding as she flicks the kitchen light on and opens the cupboard containing plasters, pills and potions. She pops a couple of paracetamol from the pack and puts them in her mouth, her head leaning her head back to keep them in as she runs water into a mug and then drinks deeply. Two won't be enough. She knows that. So she doubles the dose and then fills the kettle. The thought of a cigarette makes her feel ill, but the withdrawal symptoms are too strong. She lights up a low tar brand and draws in, shuddering as she feels the nicotine passing into her blood and taking the gnawing edge away, her slow exhalation easing her as the comforting poison reaches her brain. Her throaty cough in response is familiar, an auto-reaction to the first cigarette of the day, a short rasp resolving as quickly as it appears, the second drag dulling the urge.

She's on the third cigarette when she finishes her tea, still staring out of the unshaded window, seeing the shadows of night disappear in the brightening of the day.

She doesn't understand why the night brings out the things in her mind that should be hidden; or why they seem so vivid and yet the arrival of daylight allows them to creep back into the darkness and dull themselves while the semblance of a normal life emerges. If, that is, the current state of affairs could be deemed normal.

She had tried to go back to work a couple of times but she had clearly been struggling and her colleagues had insisted she take more time off, promising to cover her until she felt better. All of which made things worse. Who wants to stay at home, feeling guilty, staring at the four walls of what used to be a happy home but one which is full of reminders of a life that has gone forever?

She doesn't hear the floorboards creaking above her.

66

Her thoughts stop her from noticing the squeak of the stairs and she barely hears the voice behind her.

"You alright, love?"

The words linger in the air, unanswered.

He clicks the kettle and turns to face her.

"What's the matter?"

She can't say. She can't even begin to tell him.

"Jo, look I know this is incredibly hard, but we need to talk."

There's only one safe route for her now.

"Hard? Is that it?" she says flatly.

After putting the kettle on, he kneels down in front of her, taking her hands in his, trying to break the spell.

"Come on love, you can talk to me about it, you know. We're both having to deal with this, aren't we? Wouldn't it be better to do it together?"

Joanne doesn't respond. She doesn't know what to say. She knows that he is suffering and she wants to ease that, but she has a burden of guilt he has yet to know. She knows she needs help as well. She too needs to find a way to ease her own suffering.

One thing is for sure though; talking it out won't help. Not now.

How can she tell him that she thinks *she* is the reason that that Chloe has been killed?

67

By the end of the day Robinson has had enough. He stands up from Chloe's desk and pushes the chair back, lifting it slightly off the carpet and tucking it underneath.

As he goes to leave the room, he stops and leans against the door jamb, silently looking around the room, savouring the memories that are pouring back, images of her sitting at that very desk. He sees the long blonde hair, held back by a bright blue scrunchie as she focusses on her computer, pretending she hasn't heard him knocking on the door, making out that she is totally engrossed in the work; until she gives in and looks around, lifting one eyebrow in a faint imitation of someone she's seen in a film, a simple question vocalised in a single word: "And?"

He smiles longingly at the memory, imagining his reply, followed by the inevitable shrug, the 'maybes' and 'whatevers'. The sounds he hears, once the source of an intense frustration, now carries her memory so vividly; turning a forgotten frustration into a burning source of longing.

One day the room will need to be cleared. One day, perhaps in twenty years' time when he's ready to let go. Or perhaps never.

A slight push up with his arm and he turns his back on the memory, pulling the door almost shut behind him.

Then he stops. And looks back at the poster on the wall above her bed. It's a print of Gustav Klimt's 'The Kiss'. She hadn't wanted prints of boy bands or film stars, or whatever the latest influencers like to call themselves. Instead, she wanted a Klimt. She had loved that picture from the age of six, had tried to reproduce it a thousand times with particles of glitter and watercolours. Even though this was, of course, a copy, she had always been meticulous about the print; it had to be precisely level. She insisted on spirit level measurement accuracy, not simply an approximation of the eye, and would tell him to keep away from it, not wanting to spoil its perfection. One day, she used to say, she'll buy the original. Which would have been his cue to remind her to study. Once upon a time.

Today he can see the frame is slightly crooked. With an apology instinctively spoken out loud, he goes over to the frame and nudges it to the right, making it perfectly level once more. And a piece of paper slips from behind it, sliding down the wall and behind the bed.

He wants to know what she had been hiding behind the print. Pulling the bed out, it's a photograph. He reaches down, picks it up and sits on the bed as he examines the picture.

It's out of focus but he can make out the back of a head and a door of some sort beyond the head. It's obviously been taken from a distance and he doesn't think this is the entirety of the photograph. It just looks like an enlargement of a fraction of a photo that has been taken with an inadequate lens.

But there is something there. Its familiarity makes his heart lurch. He is almost certain whose head it is. No, he is almost certain, even though he cannot absolutely prove it, he just knows for sure who it is.

What he needs to know is whose door is in the picture.

And where the photo was taken from.

And why.

68

"Of course it's not me."

"Of course it fucking is. You'd have to be blind not to see it."

Joanne recoils visibly at the strength of his assertion.

"Really? Now you're resorting to abuse, are you?"

Robinson softens but only slightly.

"I just can't understand why you don't think it's you. Look, the way your hair goes down at the side here," he adds pointing at the photo he is holding out in front of them both.

"Hon, just think about it for a moment. I can understand that you think that is a picture of the back of my head. I can't agree with you because, if you thought about it for even a split-second, I never see the back of my head. And I've never seen a photo like that. Of anyone's head in a shot from that far away, let alone this imaginary me that you think is in it. Who, in their right mind, would photograph someone like that anyway? What on earth would be the point? Really? Well? Answer me?"

He cannot find an answer. He doesn't even know when Chloe got the photo.

He slumps back on the sofa, dropping the photo on the table, his hands drawing up to rub his face.

"I don't know, Jo. I just don't know."

She makes to move and hesitates, eventually turning round to face him, placing her hands on his leg and drawing in a deep breath before she speaks softly and gently:

"I know you found this picture. I know you think Chloe was hiding it for some kind of reason. But I ask you, what would be the point? She could have one of me and my face any time she wanted. And she wouldn't have to hide it either, would she? Whoever it is, whatever reason she had for keeping it, we'll never know." She pauses, then adds more: "Chloe probably wanted to try creating some different version of the kiss, a different viewpoint perhaps and that's why she kept the photo safe. Whoever was in the picture was probably an unknown, unwitting muse, who would never be seen."

Robinson's hands drop and he looks at his wife, gaunt, battered and exhausted, yet still she seeks to comfort him.

"I'm sorry. It's just..."

"I know," she says.

He watches her leave and listens to her climbing the stairs.

There is no point challenging her further now. She won't relent. He'll go up to bed with her now but not to talk. He needs the rest as much as she does.

69

Robinson puts down his coffee cup. He's got to go in to work today and he's up early, sitting fully dressed in the kitchen, thinking. Not about work. As far as he sees it, he needs to solve two problems. The first is what Samza is doing with his daughter's phone and the second is finding out what his wife is hiding.

He decides to tackle the first one first and picks up his phone.

"Hawthorns surgery."

"Oh, hi. I'd like to make an appointment with Dr Samza please."

"I'll have a look for you. When did you have in mind?"

A minute later and it is sorted. He has an appointment in the middle of the morning, the earliest time that Samza is available tomorrow. A grim smile steals across his face. He has no intention of keeping the appointment of course. But having one is important.

Before he goes to work though, he needs to tackle the other problem. Or at least take a step towards a solution. And the first step is apparent reconciliation.

"There you go," he says, putting the coffee down on the bedside table next to Joanne. She's awake, eyes open but not engaging.

"I'll be back about five," he says, leaning in to kiss her on the forehead.

Her eyes silently watch him as he leaves

On the way out, he bites back a shout to Chloe's room and tries to focus on his first day back at work. He knows it'll be difficult. He can already see people hesitating, the look in their eyes, wondering if they should mention it or not and if so what to say. In the end, it doesn't matter what they say. Nothing will be any different.

Unless he does something.

70

The house looks quiet when he returns. Curtains still open and no lights on inside.

Robinson pulls into the driveway on autopilot. He doesn't know what he's going to say or do when he gets in; all the usual niceties are trite and meaningless now. Once inside, he calls out for her. No reply. He tries again.

"Jo? Are you in?"

The silence is heavy as he waits for a reply that doesn't come. He isn't expecting anything more than an acknowledgement but hearing nothing at all is odd. The cold grip of fear reaches out and touches his heart, a sudden tightening as he joins up the dots of earlier behaviour and recent events. It takes seconds to check the downstairs rooms. But even as he is checking he knows it's pointless; if she has done anything it will be upstairs. And probably in Chloe's room.

He rushes up the stairs, stumbling at the top and desperately grabbing for the banister as his feet slip from under him, clutching tightly until he gets his feet planted on the stairs and then he continues, only more slowly. His steps falter as he reaches the closed door of Chloe's room, then he gingerly pushes on it, slowly swinging it back until he breathes a sigh of relief. She's not there.

Turning round he is on his way into the main bedroom when he notices that the carpet beneath his feet is wet. That would explain the slip on the stairs, the squidginess beneath his shoes. His face lifts as his eyes move to the bathroom door, slightly ajar, water glistening in the gap.

No.

Please God no.

71

He can't lose them both.

He calls out. Once more no reply. And he knows what is next.

Reluctantly he steps forward, pushing through the door and taking in the scene before him. An over-full bath, water everywhere, and it all has a deep pink tinge. The taps are dripping slightly and he reaches over to turn them off, seeing a piece of shining silver glistening like a tiny fish in water. His hand dips into the water, causing a current to lift and move the silvery metal and allowing him to pick it up without touching the edges.

Putting it delicately on the windowsill he sits down on the closed toilet pan, trying to decide what on earth has been going on, his logical mind holding back the panic that his emotions are surging towards.

In front of him he can see deep red marks on the door jamb and once more the icy cold finger touches his heart. He doesn't want to move. If he stays put, he won't have to face another awful reality, won't have to acknowledge the loss of all that is left to him.

But she might still be alive; he might be able to save her. Spurred on by this thought he heads out of the bathroom and back to the room where he had last kissed her, where she had lain, bereft and silent. Even as he takes a step forward, he cannot help but ask himself how could he not have thought this might happen?

The bedroom is in front of him as he approaches, trying to squint through the gap in the hinges, desperately searching for confirmation of a consequence he doesn't want to see. There is nothing obviously wrong and then he is pushing through the doorway and half-closing his eyes as he forces his head round to look at the bed, eyes opening wide as he takes in the scene. The bed is empty. Unmade but empty.

Robinson doesn't know what to do or where to look now. He slumps back against the door jamb trying to make sense of what he has seen. Why is there no blood on the door, the architrave or the handle? This is like some kind of horror movie gone wrong. How could she have disappeared? He glances to the stairway and that's when he sees the handprint. A deep red, blurred, handprint on the banister and, a little higher up, a more defined mark on the wall opposite. But she isn't downstairs. He knows that; he's checked.

Leaning over the banister he can see no more marks on the wall. But there is a dark mark on the bottom step, a footprint shape in the deep stain. A footprint facing up the stairs, repeated, more faintly two steps farther on. There must be someone else in the house. But where are they?

Then the answer becomes obvious. He made the print himself, on his way up the stairs. The blood had already been on the carpet. And it must have got there after she had been in the bath.

So she must have made it downstairs. Maybe she went outside. But where? And why wouldn't she phone for an ambulance if she had decided she wanted to live after all? Even as he asks himself the question, he knows that if you go to the trouble of doing what she had done, you don't suddenly change your mind and potter off downstairs. So maybe someone else was involved. Maybe someone else removed the body.

His head is spinning as he tries to sort out some kind of rational explanation, tries to understand how this might have happened.

His thoughts are interrupted by the sound of ringing and it takes him a moment to tune in to the noise and work out what it is.

It's the phone in his pocket.

72

2004

"Mmm, that feels good," said Matthew.

His new girlfriend smiled before she leaned over and kissed him on the lips, pushing the covers of the bed away as she lifted her leg and climbed astride him.

"So will this," she said as she slipped her t-shirt off and slid down the bed, lifting the covers to make it easier to please him, waiting until he was fully aroused before climbing on top once more and lifting her hips teasingly, sliding up and down while looking directly into his eyes, enjoying the control the movements gave her while his eyes flickered and then closed.

Moments later he rolled her onto her back and began to thrust deeply. She pulled his head down close to hers, her own eyes closing now as she worked on her own fantasy, enjoying the imagination until Matt speeded up. She knew he'd finish soon and she pushed back hard with her own hips, grinding into him, taking her own pleasure to the point she needed just as he gave a loud groan and thrust hard inside her.

Slowly his breath returned and he gently slipped out and off her, rolling onto his back and breathing deeply, making room for her to turn on her side and rest her head in the crook of his shoulder, her arm loosely draped over his chest.

"We should do that more often," she said, "Maybe even more often this morning."

"Really?"

"Complaining?"

"God, no!"

"I should hope not," she added, pushing herself out of bed and walking to the bathroom: "I'm going to shower."

His response was a grunt.

When she returned, he was gone.

"Hello?" she called.

"Yeah, I'm down here, making some coffee. Shall I bring it up or are you coming downstairs?"

"I'll come down." She sat down in front of the mirror in the bedroom and brushed her hair as she thought about the things that had happened to them both over the past twelve months.

It was his lawyer who introduced them. She might have gone for the lawyer rather than Matthew, after all he was the one she first met and he was pretty hot for a lawyer. But she was too slow. For a month or two, she was slightly miffed that her friend had become Robin's girlfriend but the more she got to know her new man, the less that mattered. Perhaps she had picked the right one after all.

At first, she had only gone out with Matthew because it had been a while since the last boyfriend and sometimes DIY just isn't enough. But the sex had been good and there was definitely some chemistry.

That was what initially connected the two of them and gradually the way they fitted together became more pragmatic; his weaknesses complemented her strengths and even though they'd had a few difficult arguments, she was settling into the idea that soon he would ask her to marry him.

She didn't know then just what that would mean for them both.

73

It was busy in the pub. She was sitting in the corner, reserving the table while Matthew had gone to get the drinks. The queue at the bar meant he was still waiting for their first drink when Robin arrived and join her at the table. Always late for everything, he surprised them this time by arriving early, presumably thanks to his new girlfriend Janine, a slender, wide-eyed girl who worked for her father. Robin, it transpired, had done some work for her father and had met her through that case- a fraud case that Robin had successfully prevented the police from pursuing. It was clear from her expression that Janine found the mixture of clever legal work and sailing close to the wind an intoxicating combination. It was also easy to see how Janine might like the intensity of his gaze, his golden-brown eyes, invitingly flecked with darker speckles that drew her in, or maybe it was the thick, wavy hair that could never quite be tamed. And an enthusiasm for running helped keep him in shape too, in sharp contrast to Matthew's gradual expansion.

Robin smiled winningly at the two of them and told them he was going to give his pal a hand, "give you two a chance to chat," he said. Code, of course, for a word or two with Matthew that he didn't want either of them to hear.

After a few minutes Robin returned, with a wide grin, waving menus and declaring himself the bearer of good tidings. When Matthew arrived with the drinks a few moments later he could see the look in Robin's eyes. Janine wasn't going to last long and Robin was ready to move on.

*

In the taxi he commented on Robin's behaviour, watching as his girlfriend's eyes sparkled:

"Flirty with me? I don't think so."

"There. In your voice. I rest my case, m'lud," said Matthew.

"I thought he was the lawyer."

"So you're not denying it then?"

"You're not worried, are you?"

"No, not really,' he said.

She pulled his hand over towards hers, taking both of her hands and enveloping his as she pulled him in towards her thighs.

"It's you I want," she whispered, letting her tongue linger across her lips. Matthew smiled back at her.

"Then you shall have me," he replied softly, leaning towards her, only to be interrupted by the taxi driver pulling sharply into the driveway.

"Keep the change," he said to the driver, handing over a twenty-pound note and getting out before walking around the car to help her out and slip his arm over her shoulders as they walked together towards the front door.

"I like you being here," said Matt. "Want to make it permanent?"

She stopped walking and turned to face him, picking out the lightness of his face in the weak reflection of a far-off streetlight.

"Is that a proposal?"

"In a way, yes. Sell your flat and let's move in here together. No point paying for two places is there?"

"You old romantic," she replied teasingly. "Perhaps. Perhaps. Now let's get in before I freeze to death."

74

"I don't know."

"Of course you do."

She hadn't meant to take the call. The phone had rung on her desk and she had picked it up without looking, swiping to answer at the very moment she looked at the caller ID and saw it was from Robin. By then it was too late; he was saying her name and she had to reply.

It started innocently enough. A chat about the night at the pub, talk about Janine's father and how Robin wanted to exit the relationship and then he asked about Matthew. She said was that he was fine and had enjoyed the evening out.

"I had a great time too. You were great company. More importantly, how are you? How's your work?"

"Not too stressful and I am still enjoying it."

"I'm glad to hear it. Talking of enjoying things…"

She could have predicted what he would say next.

"Do you think we could meet up for a drink somewhere?"

She knew. She knew what was happening and what she was agreeing to. She couldn't imagine that Robin had many boundaries and the question was full of intent. This drink was just a chance to get her on her own. And she was curious.

"I could I suppose. Maybe after work one day?"

"Tomorrow?"

"I don't know. Yes. I mean, I'll check."

"You don't need to check with anyone do you? A quick drink? Shall we say 5.30 in The Long Boot?"

"I suppose so, yes."

"Great. See you then."

The phone went dead and she took a deep breath.

She knew what would happen next.

75

He was there before her. Sitting in his car, wearing a dark blue wool suit with a powder blue tie.; a tie he had specifically chosen because an ex-girlfriend had told him how perfectly it matched his eyes and how it made her melt. If it works for one it'll work for many and he was going to use it tonight.

The moment he saw her walking down the path to the pub, he got out of his car, a midnight blue BMW M3, and held his arms out wide as she approached.

"Looking more gorgeous every day," he said as he gave her a friendly hug, pulling her in as she reached up behind his back and held his shoulders briefly. The hug might have been a second or two too long, thought Jo, even as she enjoyed the feel of his firm shoulders and the subtle smell of oud, leather and vanilla that lingered from whatever expensive eau de toilette he was wearing.

"Come on. You look like you've had a long day and need a drink," he said holding her hand and pulling her gently with him. She willingly followed and soon found herself sitting in the corner of the pub, Robin sitting close to her side. He had explained that he didn't want anyone to overhear them talking about sensitive things.

They talked about her day first and then gradually he began to charm her, taking the first verbal steps in a dance which they both knew.

She looked down at her empty glass.

"Look if we're going to take this chat any further, I'm going to need another glass of wine."

Half an hour later, the wine, his charm, his interest in her and the compliments he had so easily slipped into the conversation were having an effect. As was the feel of his hot thigh leaning against hers. She said yes when he asked her if she'd like to go back with him. She decided it wasn't going to be a relationship. It was just, she told herself, to get it out of her system. A kind of pre-hen night aberration that wouldn't be repeated and that no-one would know about.

After all, just one night won't matter, will it?

76

He lived half a mile from the pub and the moment they were inside his home, she put her hands to the back of his neck and pulled him closer, exploring with her tongue and then with her hands, an urgency to mate overcoming her inhibitions.

She pushed him back on the sofa, stepped in between his legs and undid his trousers, pulling the fabric away so she can get hold of him. Her head dropped and stayed there for a few minutes until he pushed back, and lifted up from the sofa, pressing her back onto the cushions, mumbling "Now it's your turn," and then lifting her dress up and hooking his thumbs in the waistband of her panties before lowering his head. She groaned and began to writhe, clamping down on the back of his head as she pushed back with her hips. Moments later, she shuddered and felt him move away, half-lifting, half-tilting her hips to turn her over, until her knees were on the sofa cushions and her hands on the arm. He slid inside her and began thrusting, an urgency taking over as he moved more quickly, the front of his hips slapping against her buttocks when he moved deeper inside her.

She felt the tingling inside grow, a sensitivity that had been awakened earlier now coursing through her as the sensations grew more intense, taking on a life of their own, controlling her thoughts and her movements as she pushed back, tensing, crossing her ankles and squeezing, pushing them both beyond the limits of restraint. She felt him harden still more, felt the change in rhythm, a change that set off her own anticipation and the two of them shuddered as he came inside her. The only sounds now were of his desperate breathing, fighting to fill his lungs with enough oxygen, and her spent exhalation, a bodily surrender as she loosened her grip on him, small tremors making her shudder as he barely moved inside her. She felt the moisture running away as he pulled back, slumping on to the sofa, his legs apart and she sank down, slipping her knees to one side as she rested her head against the sofa cushion. Instinctively, she turned towards him, waiting for him to move closer and draw her in. Yet he didn't move in the way she expected. He just rested his head on the cushion behind him.

"Well, that was worth waiting for," he said with a chuckle in his voice.

She didn't know what to say. She had been a willing participant but now she was flooded with regret that she hadn't been just a little bit more cautious. Despite her own willingness, she felt used and, worse, discarded in the aftermath. She knew that Robin had just wanted to have her, just wanted to bask in his ability to pull one more girl. And she had to acknowledge her part in the coupling.

She stood up, feeling the cold moisture trickle down her leg as she hurried out to the bathroom. The sound of a flush and running water and she was back in the room, rummaging for her knickers. Robin asked if she really had to go, in that tone that meant he was happy she was leaving, adding that he could always cancel his evening's plans if she wanted.

"No need," she replied. "I have to go anyway."

Moments later she was dressed and putting on her shoes.

Robin leaned forward, his hand stretched out to catch hers. He looked up at her, still working the charm as he said that he thought they shouldn't upset Matt by telling him about this.

"Okay," she said. "It stays between us."

She was safe with that. Robin wouldn't tell Matt. Unless there was a real falling out between the two of them, perhaps. Hopefully it wouldn't come to that, she told herself.

She knew though, that consequences would remain.

What she didn't realise was how significant they would be.

77

The front door closed behind her, creaking as she leaned back against it, the barrier behind her a shield against the recent past, a carapace against the guilt that was teasing the edges of her conscience. Her thighs told a different story though, the door a support to ease the trembling she still felt if she allowed the sensations in. Her knickers were damp and she needed a long hot shower; a chance to cleanse her body and soul, a way to wash the past couple of hours away, to launder them from physical memory and allow her to face the rest of the day clean.

She dropped her handbag and pushed herself up from the door, kicking off her shoes and leaving them where they fell. She would tidy up in a minute. First the shower.

*

The smell from the kitchen had begun to permeate the house: Fried spring onion, tarragon, white wine, chicken and the faintly musty smell of microwaving rice mixing with the flowery fragrance of shower gel. It smelled like an ordinary day, an ordinary evening. Slowly the ritual and routines soothed and softened, simmering and steaming away the lingering guilt. She began to think of it as a moment of weakness, or perhaps strength in taking what she wanted without regard for others, an aberration from the usual morality that ran through her. It didn't really matter. She wasn't embarking on a new relationship, she wasn't changing her life. As time ticked by, the early evening was being relegated to a soft focus, a fuzzy memory of a fantasy fulfilled and now to be forgotten.

She added a dash of cream, swirled it around the pan and then tipped the chicken onto a plate next to the rice. She picked up what remained of her glass of white wine and stepped across to the armchair that had been her mother's favourite place to sit and watch TV. Her parents had recently moved to the coast, buying a smaller property that had given her the chance to offer to take the chair into her own rented and lightly furnished flat. Settling down in front of the TV, a familiar reality show in front of her, the transformation was complete. It was literally and figuratively in her past. Something that happened in a distant place to a distant woman.

Until the phone next to her pinged. Her heart gripped tightly and her breath caught. Setting down her plate, she picked up the phone and read the message. Then she breathed more easily.

It was Matthew. Checking she was okay and to ask if she wanted to go to the new Thai restaurant opening tomorrow. Then she saw the next line.

'Think I might go for a late beer with Robin tonight.'

Nothing she could do. No need to be paranoid. All she had to do was reply normally and assume he would say nothing. Nothing direct, anyway. She wouldn't put it past Robin to be oblique, hinting without saying.

Leaving room for a convincing denial if Matthew got too close to the truth.

She just had to hope Robin wouldn't say anything.

And she didn't like just hoping.

78

Present Day

Robinson stares at the phone screen.
It's Joanne.
He swipes and holds the phone up to his ear, frowning instinctively.
"Jo? What the hell happened to you? Are you alright?"
"Nothing happened to me," replies the male voice at the other end. The voice is familiar but Robinson struggles for a moment to recognise it.
"Who?"
"It's Dr Samza here and I'm phoning about Joanne."
"Is she alright? Why are you ringing me on her phone?"
"It's okay. Don't worry. She'll be fine. But first, I think it best if you come over and collect her."
"Okay. Which hospital is she at?"
"She's not. She's at my house. Don't worry, I'll explain when you get here."
Robinson puts the phone back in his pocket and hesitates. Why would she be at the doctor's house after what looked like a suicide attempt? There is something wrong

here and he doesn't know what it is; something that doesn't quite add up. But for now, he needs to go and see what is going on.

He hurries out of the front door and runs across to the doctor's house, leaving himself breathless as he rings the doorbell, resting his hands on his knees as he draws breath, until, at last, the door opens.

79

Samza appears, pressing his finger to his lips as he pulls the door back wide to let Robinson in. Dressed in a T-shirt and jeans, with bare feet, he looks very relaxed and he puts a hand on the visitor's chest and whispers that Jo is fine, that she is sleeping. With a wave of his hand, he beckons Robinson down the hallway and into the kitchen, pointing to a chair as he shuts the kitchen door.

"Now," he says, "first things first, do you want cup of tea or coffee?"

"No. First thing is, where is Jo? What happened?"

"She is fine, I tell you. She is in the lounge sleeping for now. I've given her a sedative."

Robinson ignores him and goes to look in the lounge. He returns a moment later.

"I didn't wake her. She looks so pale though. Are you sure she'll be alright?"

"Yes."

"I wish I could talk to her. Did you have to sedate her like that? Shouldn't she go to hospital?"

"I sedated her because she needed it," says Samza icily. "Now calm down and let me tell you."

Robinson listens quietly as he hears that Jo has indeed tried to take her life by slashing her wrists, but the wounds are not deep enough to put her in any real risk and Samza has sewn and bandaged them. He tells Robinson that he just popped round to check on her, after all that had happened, and when he heard water on the stairs, he thought he should go in and check. Fortunately, the back door was open and he rushed upstairs, helped her out of the bath, wrapped her up and carried her back to his house so that he could bandage and sew.

"Why didn't you just call for an ambulance? Why would you carry my naked wife through the streets while she is dripping blood?".

"Stop being slow-witted and think about it. Firstly, she wasn't dripping blood. She was wrapped up and once I'd fixed her up, I let her take one of my track suits and gave her a sedative. But just think about it for a moment, will you? If she goes to hospital, it is recorded, it shows that she attempted suicide; there'll be a psychiatric consultation and she might even be sectioned. Is that what you would have preferred?"

"No of course not. I'm just surprised that you just happened to be there when she tried to take her own life."

"You're surprised? How do you think I felt? I had no idea that she was taking things this badly but I'm glad I decided to pop round. She is a very lucky woman."

"Well, I suppose I owe you thanks for doing what you did."

Samza smiled as he replied.

"I just did what I had to do, that's all."

Robinson struggles to balance his gratitude with the increasingly unpleasant sensation that he was being taken for a mug.

"Look, I think I'll just go home and come back when she's awake."

"Oh no, not yet," said Samza. "Why don't we upgrade the drinks? We need to talk anyway."

80

Robinson knocked back the whisky and put the glass down on the table a little too firmly.

"You need another," said the doctor, topping him up.

"How long will she sleep for?"

"Hard to be sure but with the sedative she's taken it's probably going to be a few hours. There's not much to do waiting here for her to wake up, though. Maybe you might want to clean up at home so that she doesn't have to see the evidence when she returns? I'll stay here and call you as soon as she wakes. But I would recommend you make sure you take time off to stay with her. At least until you think the danger period has passed."

"I don't know when that'll be," replies Robinson. "She has taken it really badly. In your line of work, you must know how hard it is to lose someone you love so senselessly."

"I don't think anything is senseless. Hard to comprehend, yes. Obtuse and difficult to understand, yes. But there is always a reason, a purpose, a cause and a resolution. They're just hard to discern at the time. Good will come from tragedy, they say."

Robinson doesn't agree but he can't be bothered to object. Instead, he nods and agrees that he'll go home until called. He goes into the lounge to check on the still-sleeping Jo, says goodbye, and then walks back home. Yet, as he walks, he can't shake the ever-present feeling that something isn't right.

He reaches his own front door without identifying what it might be and shakes his head. Too much drama for one day, he tells himself, pushing the door open and preparing to clean up. He starts with the carpets, using towels and cleaners to dry and clean the stain, stopping as he begins work on the footprint on the stair, his imagination running through the events as described by the doctor. He wonders why the footprint is so clearly defined. Why is it that he can see edges? Surely, if someone was rushing up the stairs, there'd be a lack of definition because the foot would be moving so quickly? He dismisses the thought as he wipes away the stains, asking himself what does it matter what speed the doctor was going? At least he got there in time. And he is grateful that Samza has saved her life. Maybe he should find a gift of some sort to say thank you. Maybe.

Forty-five minutes later and he's finished. The carpet is still damp but there are no stains, no signs of anything untoward, except for the heavy load of blood-stained towels in the washing machine, and he's wondering what he's going to do now. The only sound in the house is the rotation of towels in water, the rhythm stopping briefly and then restarting as the drum moves in the opposite direction. It reminds him of his own life. All going fine, a happily married man with a daughter he loves until it comes to a crashing halt with the death of his lovely child and now his wife is almost unrecognisable. If only he could reverse direction again and put things back to how they were.

If only.

81

The noise of his phone slowly penetrates his conscious, fighting the effects of the whiskies he'd drunk before slipping into sleep in front of the TV. Blinking, he wipes the dribble at the corners of his mouth and reaches for the phone, holding a brief conversation with the doctor before putting the phone back down and breathing a heavy sigh.

Joanne has woken up and he has to go and collect her. Robinson stands up and goes to the bathroom, leaning heavily against the sink as he waits for the water to run hot and then washes his face vigorously, trying to wipe away the leaden feeling in his blood. He slooshes a handful of water around his mouth, the stale taste reminding him that he really does need to clean his teeth before he goes.

It's dark as he makes his way to the doctor's house, the wind is stronger than earlier and he feels a chill seeping through the thin jacket he is wearing. Hurrying to the front door, he is forced to squint as the two bright but misaligned LEDs by the front door activate when he steps within range, the light sharpening his headache and making him feel momentarily nauseous. His hand reaches out to the bell, but the door is opened before he can press the button.

"Hi," says the doctor, "she's ready for you," he says, moving back into the hall as Jo steps forward, her eyes focussed on the doorstep in front of her rather than looking up at her husband. She reaches out a bandaged arm to steady herself as she puts a foot out and Robinson holds her elbow, putting his other arm around her shoulder. She moves unsteadily closer.

"The sedative is still working a bit," says the doctor, "so be careful."

Robinson doesn't answer immediately, making sure she is stable enough to start walking up the driveway. He looks behind him at the man standing in the doorway and calls out a loud thank you just in time to see the door close and the outside lights go off. But not before he has seen it. And the noise of the thing that's bugging him grows louder.

It was the doorway.

The angle.

He's seen it before.

In the photo.

82

Samza watches from the front window as Robinson and Joanne stumble home, his eyes narrowing as he sees the man turn and look back at the house once more. He doesn't know exactly why but it makes him suspicious. And more than that, the secretary at the surgery had told the doctor that Robinson was coming to see him the next day. Odd then that he hadn't mentioned anything, not even to postpone the appointment. Maybe nothing conclusive in itself, but Samza's instincts are good. Perhaps Robinson has started to put some things together?

He shakes his head as he dismisses the idea. There is no way that can be happening. Something else is going on.

Now he has to get on with the work he needs to finish. He is going through a number of medical records seeking 'suitable' candidates for a new drugs trial. He simply provides the information and then others do the contacting and contracting.

He's less happy about the alteration of some medical records, post hoc. Not that he has any moral objection, after all these people could check the data if they wanted and they don't, so it's their problem. No, he is more concerned that there will be traceability. He doesn't use his own access passwords, that's for sure but, though it is admittedly hard, given his use of TOR, proxy servers and disguised IP addresses, it still might be possible to link it to his computer. He limits the risk still further by buying a computer with cash and replacing it every 6 months, enough, he thinks, to keep him in the clear.

Even with that risk, or, more accurately perhaps, because of the risk, it pays well. Last year he pulled in nearly £100,000 tax free in addition to his GP pay. And that's twice what it was the year before. If he didn't need the job for access to records, and basic credibility, he wouldn't see any patients as a GP. But his continued status, as well as medical knowledge, makes him much more useful than the teenager hacking from abroad that other organisations might use.

He rubs his eyes to ease the discomfort of the screen's blue light burning into his tired retinas. This work needs to be done by morning. He has promised and notwithstanding his unexpected mercy work, he knows that with these people you don't fail to deliver. They had shown him a video of what happened to his predecessor. The woman had not been convicted in a court of law but had attempted to reduce her likely sentence by co-operating with the authorites. She had been given bail but she didn't make her final appearance at the court.

She had, according to the rumour mill, taken flight and was believed to be in Mexico or Brazil. Samza knew better. She was deep in an Essex estuary. At least most of her body was. The identifiable parts had been removed and burned. Or rather burned and then removed once she had been sufficiently repentant.

The thought spurs him on.

83

She is sleeping once more. This time in her own bed, the covers tucked up around her, her breathing soft, gentle, rhythmic.

Unlike Robinson's. He cannot sleep. It's not just the effect of alcohol wearing off. He is exhausted but even so his mind won't stop racing. He can't explain the links he has found and knows he needs to ask Jo about it. But he hasn't got a clue how to do it without causing a fearsome reaction. If he pushes her too hard then she might try another suicide. If he leaves it, then he may never know what has been going on.

But his mind is putting it all together: Her actions. The doctor's responses. The photograph. It's obvious. She's been seeing the doctor.

He doesn't know when it all started but the more he thinks about it, it's the only thing that makes sense. But why the suicide attempt? And to add confusion to his analysis, Samza wasn't acting like a man carrying on an affair with his wife. It didn't add up. Yet what other explanation is there?

Robinson's mind is churning, sending fear, anxiety and adrenaline to every part of his body. His heart pounds as he realises that she might have been cheating on him since even before Chloe died.

He knows if he doesn't get this under control quickly, he's going to go under, going to start drinking and then things will be worse. They survived a time, long ago, when they were both drinking heavily and Robinson knows it can't happen again.

He tells himself to stop thinking, to calm down, to get some sleep and then, in the morning, when he is feeling better, he'll be able to think about it calmly and rationally. Maybe there'll be a perfectly logical explanation that he hasn't thought of. Maybe he's making Olympic-sized jumps to conclusions that won't hold up in the cold light of day.

He takes a deep breath. His eyes close and he works his way round his body, tensing and then deliberately relaxing muscle groups, imagining each group bathed in the warmth of a tropical sun; healing and soothing heat flowing over his body. His breathing slows and he begins to slip into the darkness even as the question returns to his mind.

"But what if she *is* cheating?"

84

Robinson checks his watch once more. It is precisely one minute later than last time he looked. And he knows he's only doing it to delay his planned move.

"I'm just going for a walk," he calls out to Joanne, pulling the front door behind him before she can reply. As he walks down the driveway and along the road, he's not so sure that this is a good idea. Samza will be out but there may be other neighbours watching. Taking a deep breath as he walks, he tells himself to calm down. He's only going to look. Best try and look nonchalant and no-one will think anything of it. He fights the urge to look around constantly, trying to avoid doing something that will draw attention to him. He wants to look just like a neighbour going round to have a friendly chat with another neighbour.

Reaching Samza's house he rings the bell and steps back to wait, counting to twenty before he rings again, certain that there will be no response, especially as Samza should be waiting for him to appear at the surgery. This time he does a quiet 360 turn, ostensibly an impatient man looking at his watch, as if there's an appointment to be kept, but in truth a chance to check no-one is watching.

Just in case, he pulls his phone out of his jacket and pretends to take a call, looking at the front window, raising a thumb and nodding and then going to the side gate. He pushes the thumb latch and rattles the door. It's bolted but the way the door responds to his shaking makes it clear the bolt is at the top. A stretch and then he's in.

Robinson peers into the back door. No sign of movement here or in any of the ground floor windows, all of which are tightly closed. He returns to the back door and tries the handle. Locked.

Shit.

He looks around for something suitable to smash the window with but the only items in reach are a plastic bin and a couple of chairs. The chairs are white painted, designed to look Victorian in style. Which means they'll be cast iron. Perfect.

He looks around again, an anxiety prickling at his senses, checking to see there is no-one around to see him. He takes a step towards the chair and looks up at the house, checking the windows above for any sign of life.

Then he sees the CCTV camera, high up on the wall overlooking the back door.

Fuck.

Not only has he been filmed checking out the house, he has even turned his face full on to the camera. So Samza will see what he's done and who he is. There's no hiding it. Fuck.

Then he has an idea. Two minutes later he's back home, his heart rate slowing as the answer becomes clear in his mind. The tension eases and a wave of fatigue strikes.

He needs to hold his nerve but it should work.

85

In the surgery, Samza presses the buzzer for the next patient. He waits a minute and then presses again. How can people be so stupid? he thinks. There's a bloody great scrolling notice board beeping and calling them in, but still they don't get the message. He doesn't have time for this pointless hanging around. He presses again, giving the patient one last try before he'll move on.

There's a brief knock at the door and it pushes open wide, followed by Dan Jones. Not the patient he expected.

Pleasantries exchanged, Samza wants to get to the point.

"So Dan, what's up?"

Jones rubs his nose before sitting down in the patient chair. Samza notices the way Jones slyly wipes his hand on the arm of the chair as he speaks.

"I need help for stress. I'm under a lot of pressure from the bank. You won't know but I took out quite a loan to update the parlour- make it more visitor friendly and all that, not to mention more hygienic. Anyhow, the money isn't coming in fast enough to keep up. People need to pay more for their funerals, I suppose. Or I need more people dying. Maybe another pandemic wave would do the job."

"Well I can't exactly give people fatal injections to order, you know. Hippocratic oath and all that, eh?" Samza replied.

"I know that. Maybe you can just give me some tablets to help while I try to find a way to increase turnover. Some places are doing their own flowers, offering grief counselling and the like. I've tried adding extras and fancy bits but I'm he just not making enough at the end of the day. I reckon I've got six months to get the numbers sorted or I'll be on the street. And that means being booted out of the company-owned flat. And my Mrs isn't too happy either, I can tell you that."

"Well, I can give you some pills I suppose, although that won't solve the problem, which is what you really need to do."

"I bloody know that."

Well, if you're going to be abusive..."

"No look sorry doc. I didn't mean it. It's just that..."

Jones twisted his hands, waiting for a push. Samza was curious to find out what was really on Jones's mind, so he gave a little help. He raised his hand and swatted away the sharp comment.

"Don't worry about it. Tell me, what else were you thinking?"

"Well, it's just that... you do know when people are going to die, don't you?"

"Not for sure, obviously."

"Yes, but you'll have a good idea in many cases. And if it's going to happen soon you could put in a good word for me, couldn't you?"

Samza pushes back from the desk and looks more closely at the man in front of him.

He is well into his sixties; an average height but portly as a result of a lifetime of over-indulgence. He has a weathered face, the scar from a melanoma removal still clearly visible, as are the red veins of a drinker's nose. Samza could put the man at the top of his list. Except that he knows the combination of aspirin, betablockers and statins will probably keep him going for a while longer. What matters though is not the man's health but whether he can be trusted.

"But that would be unethical," he says. "Why on earth would you come to me with such an idea?"

86

"Ah well now, forgive me, I should have mentioned that earlier, I suppose. I was talking with the Mike Williams, the police superintendent, about the business and how things were getting tricky. I thought he might be able to point me to someone who would help me out and he suggested I come see you. He told me he knew you very well and you were a man I could trust. So here I am."

The doctor watched carefully. No non-verbal leakage, no micro-expressions to indicate the man wasn't being truthful. And Jones will know that the story could be checked.

"Okay. Well, let me see, what if I could do better than that?"

"What do you mean?"

"Well, if I were to provide you with timescales of likely deaths and addresses of the patients, then you could market to them directly. I wouldn't be overtly involved. You get the leads. Then the business. And all I ask for is a small fee."

"How small?"

"Let's say £100 for each success."

"Doesn't sound that small to me."

Samza leans forward.

"What's an average funeral cost? Thousands? Seems small enough to me."

"Well, possibly, but only if it's to be paid when I've done the funeral."

Samza decided it's time to spice it up.

"Let me put it this way. If I could get you advance notice of likely deaths in a radius of fifty miles from here, which would be thousands each year, would you be interested?"

Jones' face breaks into a smile.

"I think we could come to an agreement on that."

Jones stands up, offering his hand out to the doctor. He takes it and they shake on the deal.

"Pop in next week and we'll make a start," says the doctor, guiding Jones out of the office and closing the door behind him.

By the time he gets back to his desk, Samza is already planning how he's going to get the data onto a USB ready for next week. At this rate, he'll retire in a couple of years. Once he's worked out how to extricate himself from under the control, or more specifically, the threat to life from the people he has been working with.

87

It's past dark by the time Samza gets home. He knows the best way to continue with his extra-curricular work is to show competence in the day job and avoid any unnecessary scrutiny, even if that does mean long hours sometimes.

Worse yet, he's still got more work to do for his private employers.

He makes himself a coffee and sips on it as he sits at his computer and thinks about what he's going to do first. A small blue light is blinking to the right of his screen, telling him that the CCTV had been activated during the day. He opens the application out of habit, expecting to see another bloody fox sniffing around. What he does see surprises him. Robinson walking around the house and testing the doors. Samza leans forward, focussing intently on the man's movement, his pulse rising as it becomes clearer that the man is trying to break in. The camera picks out him looking up directly at the lens, and then, unexpectedly, the man in the video lifts his hand, waves and raises his thumb to gesture okay. What the hell does that mean?

A replay of the entire footage changes nothing. Why was he looking? And why did he give a thumbs up?

Samza orders his food online as he thinks about the best way to deal with this. He comes to the conclusion that the only way is to confront Robinson directly; and perhaps have a go about the 'fake' appointment too. He smiles as he decides it's time to make a home visit. He'll claim to be concerned for Joanne first of course. The sure sign of a kind, considerate family doctor.

88

His curry tastes blander than usual. The doctor has drunk half a beer but that doesn't excuse the lack of taste. The frustration with the food is matched by his frustration at the discussion with Robinson.

When Samza had asked after Joanne, Robinson had claimed she was asleep and he wouldn't wake her. It was an obvious lie, made more obvious by the fact that she had been standing at the top of the stairs, unseen by her husband, frowning and waving Samza away. Somewhat superficially, Samza had told Robinson to pass on his best wishes and explained he was always available to help either of them.

Then he had turned to Robinson himself, asking if the man was well, given his failure to attend the surgery that day. Caught in another lie, Robinson blustered, claiming he had forgotten but would rebook.

"Oh really? Anyway, what was the appointment for? Are you unwell?"

"Not really," said Robinson, "I just wanted to talk about vaccinations that's all."

Samza decided not to demolish the argument on his doorstep. Maybe it's best if

Robinson thinks he has been believed. Why give away knowledge until you need to?

"Okay, well you can always pop in again."

Samza turned to leave before pausing and turning back round.

"I just wanted to ask something. Why were you wandering around the outside of my house earlier?"

Robinson didn't bat an eyelid.

"I thought I heard some glass smashing and wanted to check it out. Couldn't see anyone so I waved at your camera to let you know it was all okay. I'm glad you saw the wave- I wasn't sure it wasn't a fake CCTV camera."

Samza nodded. It was impossible to prove these were lies but he knew. The man had been trying to break in and it was bound to be in connection with Chloe in some way.

Happily, Samza told himself, Robinson can't know the full picture. Otherwise he might well have been more determined to break in. Fortunately, the doctor knows he has options to stop him if he tries.

Neither of them had spoken for a moment, the doctor using the silence to make his point and then he had once again offered his help to Jo whenever needed and left.

He had made it home just in time to catch the delivery driver with his supper.

Now the doctor finishes the last of the curry and pushes it away, drinking the remains of the beer in the glass, wiping his mouth and feeling the uncomfortable expansion of his stomach now accommodating his over-sized meal. He belches and puts his hands on either side of his belly, groaning slightly as he ponders his interaction with Robinson. It's clear that the man still doesn't have a clue about Chloe or his wife.

Time, he decides, to step back a little. The more he interacts with them, the greater the danger that they might piece things together. And if the man continues to sniff around, he'll get a shock he's not expecting.

Confident that he is not at risk for now in any event, Samza stands to clear the dishes away and get back to his work in the study.

The Robinsons are not the only game in town.

89

It is morning the following day, and Robinson has finally gone to work. It had taken half an hour of reassurance before he had accepted that Joanne wasn't going to try and kill herself again, that she was fine and that he could safely go to work.

"Ring me if you need anything," he said as he left, continuing to make 'call me' signals as he climbed into the car and then drove off.

Joanne runs over the road and rings on the doorbell of the doctor's house. The door is opened and Samza looks out and then steps back, inviting her in and closing the front door behind her. She doesn't wait, walking straight through to the lounge and sitting down in the brown leather Eames armchair that backs onto the front window.

"Well, did you tell him?"

"Of course, I didn't say anything. I am a doctor and I have an ethical obligation for confidentiality, don't I?"

The doctor focusses on projecting professional certainty while Joanne looks sceptically at him before she explains the purpose of her visit.

"I know he thinks he is on to something."

"Why do you say that?"

"He has been upstairs in her room for hours over the last week, sorting through her PC, checking her email accounts and Instagram feed. And I can tell by the way he's behaving, he's suspicious."

"You're being overly sensitive. He hasn't said anything to me," said Samza, wanting to push the discussion along. "Can we get to the point?"

"He has seen a photo of me going into your house."

Samza sighed impatiently.

"Which could be for any number of reasons. It's not a cause for concern."

"But it is a worry."

"Why?"

"Because I denied it was me and I know he doesn't believe me."

"So what? He doesn't know for sure or he wouldn't have asked you."

Joanne knows that the doctor hasn't really understood. He doesn't know Robinson like she does; once he's convinced, you need a nuclear device to part him from his conviction.

Samza has had enough.

"Look, why don't you tell him it was you? Tell him one of your friends was having menstrual problems and you wanted advice. Or tell him that you wanted to ask about vaccines. Maybe you thought you could save having to get a surgery appointment. Or tell him you were thinking about having a street party and wanted to know if I'd join in."

She knows Samza isn't treating it seriously enough.

"Just promise me," she says, her voice dropping in volume, "promise me that he won't be able to find anything out about...you know."

"Joanne, all of that is in medically secure files and there's no way he can get to it. Really, don't worry. Now, if you don't mind, I've got things to get on with."

90

He's found a document marked 'Mama Bear'.

It's the name she would sometimes call her mother, whenever she was being affectionate. He doesn't really want to open it. It'll just remind him of the relationship between the two of them. His eyes moisten as he tries to hold back the thought that it's never going to be there again. Swallowing, he knows he has to carry on and open it. For Chloe's sake.

Robinson clicks to open it and the first line tightens his heart.

Mama bear is keeping secrets.
Tuesday 8th 4.07pm 35 minutes
Wednesday 16th 5.09 pm 46 minutes.
Monday 21st 1.15pm 51 minutes.
Photo.
Why? Must get closer.
Thursday 24th. Mama bear denies anything going on. Says just chatting. Seems like a nice man. Don't tell father, he'll be jealous.

He sits back and feel his stomach twisting.

91

Two months earlier

It is her.

The doctor is sure of it. At first there was only a vague inkling that she was the one. Time has passed for both of them but though he has filled out, lost hair and grown a beard, she has barely changed from the lithe, full-breasted woman he remembers. The hair is different of course and lines have formed, but none that shift his certainty that this is the one.

The pleasure is all the greater because she clearly has no clue. No idea that he was one of her clients, no idea that the gangly awkward teen had grown up. He has the advantage of not being her first, and so he is not especially memorable. She, however, was his first.

And now she is here, sitting in his consulting room.

This could be fun. This will be fun. But first, he wants to see why she is here.

"So how can I help you," he glances down to search for her name, "Mrs er Robinson?"

"It's er...kind of a difficult thing to talk about."

Samza decides to be suitably reassuring.

"That's okay. I'm used to hearing all sorts of things from patients and it would be very surprising if I haven't had a patient with a similar issue before. And it's all completely confidential. So just relax, take your time, and tell me how I can help."

"Well, I'm not ill. It's that I need to find something out, something medical I suppose."

"Go on."

"I er look, my husband won't get to find out about this will he?"

"No, of course not. I would only discuss anything you say today if you expressly gave me your permission, Otherwise, he won't know."

This really is going to be fun, thinks the doctor.

"It's about my daughter really."

"Your daughter?"

"Yes. Well, no. It's her father. Probably."

"You're not making much sense, I'm afraid. Can you explain?"

It's just that there is something I'm worried about. Have been for ages to be honest. And I need to have an answer. But discreetly. I really don't want him to know."

92

Samza is beginning to understand.

"What happened?"

"It's something I shouldn't have done. It's really embarrassing to admit, to be honest. I wish I hadn't done it but it was just once. It just happened. I know it's all a bit of a cliché and I don't really know why I did it," she said, taking a deep breath and then letting the words spill out: "I think that Chloe may be someone else's daughter."

"I think I understand, but what exactly would you like me to do?" asks the doctor.

"Simple. I just want to know for sure."

"I see. Well, this is very difficult ethically, as you might imagine. Have you spoken to your daughter to see whether she wants to know?"

"God no. I don't want her to know anything about it unless she really needs to. If the result isn't what I want then maybe the time will be right but for now, I would prefer to keep this just between us."

"I'm not sure I can help then. There is a real dilemma here. It's Chloe's life, her future that has to be considered."

"But it's my past."

"That's true and that is the point. It's the past."

"And it affects my present and very possibly my future too."

"That again is true."

Samza lifts his hand to his chin, stroking his beard for a moment.

"Look, this is more complicated than that too. I need to think about whether your husband really ought to know," he holds up a hand to stop her imminent protest, "but I won't tell him of course. The thing is that even if I could see a way through the ethical part, I know this isn't something you can have done on the NHS. Unless of course there were some genetic illness that needed to be addressed?"

"Not that I know of."

"So, in that case, as an NHS doctor there isn't really much I can do."

His hands drop to the surface of the desk and he makes as if to push himself up, stopping at the last moment and looking back at her. "However, I do run some private clinics occasionally and since you're a near neighbour, perhaps you might like to do this in a more delicate way? It won't take long and it will remain very discreet. Best of all, perhaps, it won't show on any of your medical records and so your privacy is completely protected."

"Well that sounds fine but how much is it?"

"That depends a little on the type of test and speed but don't worry, it's not expensive. I can get a special rate and I won't charge for my time either."

"Thanks. So er…"

"Look why don't you call round to my house one afternoon when it suits you? Let me just tell you what you need to do for now and I'll give you my mobile number so you can arrange a time to come over."

93

The door opens slowly and Samza appears, still half-reading a set of medical papers as he swings the door open. He looks up and sees her; a nervous, hesitant and slightly guilty look about her as she says hello and reminds him of the appointment.

"Oh, yes, I'm sorry", he says, pretending to have forgotten it is today. Please, come on in. It's the door to the right at the end of the hallway."

She walks to the study and stands awkwardly in the doorway until he catches up and, with outstretched hand, indicates the armchair for her to sit down.

"So, Joanne, let's see. Have you brought everything with you?"

"I think so. I've got samples of her hair and his," she says handing over two envelopes.

"That's great. We can certainly get a result with that but of course, it won't confirm; it will only eliminate."

"Yes, I know, I've been thinking about that. I don't have the sample of DNA that you'll need for that, but maybe we should check this first. After all, I can't be absolutely certain that my husband isn't Chloe's father."

"Well, you will be once we've done the analysis. But I need to ask you some questions about your medical history as well."

"Why would you need that for a DNA test?"

"It's just that as part of the research protocols they like to know details, in case there is a genetic link or predisposition to both illness and life events that they might pick up. As you'll see from the forms, in exchange for absolute anonymity they ask to use your data to help identify and ultimately find ways to treat illnesses and conditions that might be predictable. And of course, it sometimes happens, rarely I must say, that the test reveals something that could be relevant to your medical status. And any data you provide can help with that."

"Well, alright then. Ask away."

Samza rattled through a list of childhood illnesses first, asking if she remembers having had any of them.

"I think I've got that right, although wouldn't my medical records show all this anyway?"

The doctor smiled as he made reassuring noises:

"I'm sure you've remembered everything but to answer your question directly, your records wouldn't necessarily pick all illnesses up. Sometimes they just aren't worth reporting to the doctor- we've all had flu and not troubled the GP, haven't we? Sometimes though, people's records get lost, even in this day and age, and so it's always better to ask about all the usual stuff.

"As opposed to the unusual," she joked.

"Yes," he said taking her seriously, "I was going to come on to that."

Jo frowned. This sounded ominous.

"I need to ask you about an area of life that people often feel uncomfortable discussing, but which can prove vital to DNA researchers. So forgive me if these questions seem intrusive, but they are there for a purpose."

"And if I don't?"

"The test will be more expensive. Your data is what makes it cheaper. And anyway, they aren't that intrusive. Not for most people anyway."

94

"I don't think I want to answer that kind of question," said Jo. "I don't have to, do I?"

"No, of course not. But there is a discount on the test, quite a good discount, if you do and, as I say, you may get some reassuring data, based on your DNA and what we know about genetic predisposition."

"Well, let's see."

"Okay. The questions are generally about your sexual activity."

"Is that relevant?"

"Well," said Samza, "you know for example that having Human Papilloma Virus, HPV, which is believed to cause cancer of the cervix, is dependent upon the sex life of the individual. At its most extreme, of course, no sex means no HPV and so that's why this is part of the research. And, as I say, the questions and your answers are entirely confidential and anonymised once they go into the system. You become a number and no-one will be able to identify you specifically from that data."

"Except you."

"Well, not even me. I will hear your answers now, and you are protected in this by my duty of confidentiality, but your data is anonymised from the moment it goes in the machine. So it's quite safe, believe me."

Jo twists her hands together as she hesitates. Samza says nothing. He knows she'll answer and he's looking forward to it. Yet he says nothing, savouring the hesitancy and the information to come.

Her eyes lift and she looks up at him and nods.

Samza rearranges his spectacles as he looks at the sheet of paper in his hand.

"Let's see now. How many sexual partners have you had?"

"I er…"

"Is it fewer than ten, ten to twenty, twenty to forty or more?"

"More."

"Have you ever been paid for sex?"

"I don't see how that…"

"Well, it seems that often people who have been paid for sex have often been more careful with partners- more use of condoms and such like, so it is relevant. It's a more sensible, practical attitude to sex."

"Well, I er, when I was a student, it was tough, you know. I didn't have much money and I just thought that people do it for love or fun anyway, so why not get paid to help me pay my way through university? So I did take money a few times."

Samza tried to ask the next question in as flat a tone as possible, not wishing to betray the pleasure he was getting from her obvious discomfort.

"Were there any special preferences? BDSM, that kind of thing, or more standard sexual practice?"

Jo's head moves back as she takes in the question.

"Pardon?"

"It's only a risk related aspect that's all. Dangers of infection and all that."

"Well, it was just normal sex but I'm not sure this is in anyway relevant you know?"

"Okay, I completely understand your point of view. This is the last question and it is a relevant one."

He pauses briefly, relishing the gritty intimacy of the discussion. Samza puts on a concerned voice, enjoying the fact that she seems oblivious.

95

Joanne frowns as he asks the question.

"Have you had any sexually transmitted infections?"

"No, I haven't. At least, none that I have ever been aware of."

"They don't all show symptoms but still." He sighs as she leaves the issue hanging. "Well," he adds, 'that's it for the questionnaire. If you can let me have the £250 for the test, then I can let you go and put all the info into the computer without you having to wait for me."

She hands over five fifty pound notes and asks when the results will be back. A week. Not too long to wait, she thinks. And at least then she'll know for sure.

"Oh and one more thing. Do you have a photo of your husband? It often helps to be absolutely sure who I am talking to in cases like this. Helps me to maintain an absolute confidentiality and avoid accidental disclosures."

"Oh, er yes, I do. I have one here," she says, flicking through her phone for a suitable image and turning the phone to face Samza when she is satisfied.

He doesn't react when he sees the photo. But there is no doubt. He is certain. He smiles as he hands the phone back to her. He doesn't yet know exactly how it will happen but he has been given the opportunity he has always wanted. All he needs now is a little time to work it through properly.

Samza closes the door behind her and smiles. She clearly doesn't recognise him. Or at least if she does, and he saw no sign of it in her face, then she's never going to admit it. They were both much younger then. He remembered she barely looked at him and he certainly didn't pay a great deal of attention to her face. He remembers very clearly how he tried to avoid eye contact, tried to hide the embarrassment by pretending that the social niceties didn't matter.

It had been a brief encounter, too brief perhaps, but at least it kept his anonymity. And the fact that she doesn't remember is one less thing to worry about. One less link to connect her to him.

It isn't Jo's fault anyway. She is just collateral, as the military might say. An innocent, well not quite so innocent perhaps, but an innocent with a past that has no bearing on today. Except as an opportunity and as an unwitting participant in the balancing of the books.

For today, he already knows what the results will say. There's only one reason she had the test without her husband's knowledge; in her heart of hearts, she already knows the truth too. And if the daughter is someone else's it won't matter. It's a delicious irony that Jo isn't the only one who wants to protect the illusion that her husband is Chloe's father. Samza wants to keep the secret too. For, he tells himself, pain stems from belief, not from fact.

And there is of course a financial reward for the doctor. Ironically her fear that he might let out a secret, a secret he actually wants to keep, will cost her dearly.

It's enough to make him smile broadly.

And move on with his plan.

96

She walks hurriedly away from the house, glancing around her to see if anyone is watching her, aware that visiting him is risky but she is unable to avoid it. Most of all, she doesn't want Chloe to know she's been there.

But Chloe is quietly watching from her mother's bedroom window. She had seen her mother in the distance as she came back home, had seen her hurry down the path and go into the doctor's house. For a moment she was tempted to go up to the door and knock loudly, to challenge her mother as to what she was doing. Or, more accurately, to see if there was sufficient proof when the door opened. But her nerve had failed and she had chosen to carry on home and set up in her mother's room to watch for an exit.

Her phone was trained on the house, camera ready to capture evidence that she would use to confront her mother. Evidence that she would threaten to give to her father if Jo wasn't truthful. Now she appears and Chloe begins to record, just as her mother turns back to say something to the doctor. The goodbye between them seems perfectly proper, no sign of an intimate relationship but, she tells herself, there wouldn't be if they were saying goodbye publicly, would there? Pulling back behind the bedroom curtains now, Chloe turns her phone off and hurries to her own bedroom, putting music on and shutting the door, swiftly ditching her school clothes and dressing casually. She hears a door slam downstairs and her mother calling out to her.

Chloe shouts out that she is upstairs and will be down in a minute, buying some time while she tries to figure out if her mother really is having an affair or not. She wasn't in there long but that doesn't really mean much. Her mother looked slightly relieved when she left but what can that mean anyway? The thing that is certain is that there is a secret.

And there is no easy way to get someone to disclose a secret if they don't want to.

Maybe, she thinks, the best way to deal with this is just to confront her mother directly.

97

"I didn't see you come home," says Joanne, standing by the kitchen door, cigarette in hand, looking out to the garden but very aware of Chloe's presence.

"No, it was an early finish today. And I wanted to come home because I've got loads of homework to do and I wanted to get started."

"You must be the only teenager ever to have said that."

"God Mum, that's so funny. Not."

Chloe saw her mother's shoulders lift slightly and fall, an acknowledgement.

"Anyway Mum, I was upstairs, by the landing, and when I looked out of the window, I saw you coming out of the doctor's house?"

She left the question hanging, watching her mother's back closely but there was no reaction. No response either.

"Mum?"

Joanne turns round and looks blankly at Chloe, taking a drag, her eyes crinkling as the smoke drifts upwards, a look that dares Chloe to take the next step.

"What?"

"The doctor's house."

"I think the answer is in the question. It was the doctor's house."

"For God's sake mum, I know that."

"Well, you should know then that conversations with doctors are confidential."

"I know that too, but why are you seeing him at home and not the surgery?"

Joanne is ready for this one.

"Have you tried booking an appointment nowadays?"

Chloe decides to deal with the medical argument first, rather than go straight for the affair theory.

"Yeah, but I don't get why it's urgent enough for him to see you at his house and not urgent enough to see you at the surgery. And what's wrong anyway?"

Intelligence is usually a blessing, thinks Jo, except when it's being shown by an inquisitive daughter.

"Look, it's confidential, okay? Nothing wrong, no need to be concerned and no need to get involved."

This provokes the expected response; Chloe's words being shouted out as she runs out of the kitchen and back upstairs.

"SORREE! Only trying to care about my mother. Why can't you just be a half-decent human being?"

The door slams behind her and Chloe throws herself on the bed. From feeling as though she had the perfect question to being dismissed out of hand has been a shock. It leaves her with no way to approach the subject of an affair and does nothing to reassure her about her mother's health. For a moment she wonders whether there is something smoking related to worry about but surely that would need equipment, hospitals and x-rays? And anyway, she doesn't look ill. Chloe opens her phone and looks once more at the photos she took and her heart sinks. What she expects to see are clear pictures. There aren't any. There is only one that might be good enough; the image picking up the back of her mother's head as she is leaving. Not enough but the start of what might be the proof she is looking for. Chloe is about to delete the shot when a thought occurs to her. Her printer whirrs into life and she tucks the printed photo behind a picture frame, somewhere her mother won't see it.

98

Jo can see him out of the corner of her eye. He shifts in his seat again. She knows he's bored and she knows why. The TV programme is not his choice. It's hers. One she knew he'd hate. Unfortunately, he has decided that it is better to sit and suffer than to object and stoke what he thinks would be an inevitable row.

This time he is wrong. She needs him out of the room and preferably out of the house.

"Oh, for fuck's sake. Just go, won't you?"

"What?"

"I can see you don't like this, so why don't you just go out for a walk."

Robinson doesn't argue and she hears the front door slam a minute later. Just in time. It's nine o'clock and this is when she is expecting the call. Neurotically checking the time once more, she stares at the phone, waiting, willing it to ring. But there is nothing. She wants to dial his number herself but, even as she brings the phone closer, she knows she won't have the nerve to phone him. So she stares. And jumps sharply when it bursts into life, an insistent ring demanding to be answered.

Yet she hesitates. As much as she is expecting the call, she doesn't want to face it. She doesn't want to hear the result. It rings another five times and she answers, taking a deep breath before speaking:

"Hi."

"Hi Joanne. It's Doctor Samza." A pause, then: "I've got the results for you. Look I won't go into the technical details but in essence I can confirm that Chloe is *not* your husband's daughter."

Joanne is silent as her fears are confirmed. She is beginning to wish she hadn't started this. What had she been thinking? Maybe she could have just left it and lived with the uncertainty. But she knows there is a reason she didn't want to leave it.

Her mind comes back to the call.

"As we discussed," says Samza, "because I only had the two samples, I can't tell you who *is* the father, but I suspect you already know the answer to that question, don't you?"

Joanne is silent as a deep regret steals over her, as she began to deal with the reality. She used to be able to push guilt and sorrow away, leaving it all in the realm of the hypothetical. She had nearly convinced herself that Robinson is the father. And he loves the girl as much as any father can. So that makes him the father, doesn't it? Except for the biology. Except for the reality that the real father is someone else. Someone who doesn't yet know that Chloe is his daughter. Should she tell the biological father now? Now that the excuses are gone?

And that idea is not without risk or consequence.

The doctor continues: "Why don't you come and see me when you have had a chance to digest the news and we can talk about what has to be done next."

She wants Samza off the phone now.

"Look, I've got to go, Thanks for phoning. Gotta go. Bye."

She doesn't see the smile at the other end of the line, doesn't know the satisfaction the news has given him.

She puts the phone down and lights a cigarette, drawing in a long first drag and exhaling slowly, the clouds of swirling smoke a metaphor for the indecision in her mind.

The next steps needed thinking about.

99

Present day.

The two of them are sitting in the front room. Joanne has a nearly empty glass of vodka and tonic in front of her and a cigarette in her hand. Robinson has chosen not to drink alcohol and is nursing a cup of coffee.

The conversation has drifted inevitably to Chloe and her phone and the conversation is going round in circles. He is making the point that her phone seems to have disappeared at the time of the accident and given its presence in the doctor's hallway and the way the man is behaving, he is clearly involved. Joanne isn't acknowledging anything that he says; she just listens silently without moving, her eyes blanking him, until he finishes. Then she speaks.

"You do know he could simply have found the phone, don't you? It could easily have fallen out when he was helping her, when she..."

"So why didn't he give it to us? Why wasn't it returned with the rest of her things?"

"I don't know. Could be any number of reasons."

"Like what?"

Her voice shortens: "I don't know. Why don't you just ask him?"

"I did."

"And?"

"He told me it wasn't her phone."

"Well, there you are then."

This is going nowhere. He needs proof to make his point. One thing is for sure; Joanne isn't going to help him. So he'll have to do it on his own. He decides to tone it down for now, deciding too against mentioning 'Mama Bear'. if Joanne slashes her wrists after Chloe's accidental death, he thinks, it's likely that she'll do something worse if she thinks she's to blame. So he holds it back and tries to find a middle ground.

"Perhaps it's time to let it go," he says, "it won't change anything. It's only a phone and, as you say, there could be any number of reasons."

Jo nods silently and lights another cigarette, standing up and walking to the front window, looking out towards the doctor's house.

"You know," she says, "we should do everything we can to honour and remember her life, not obsess about her death or anything else that we can't change."

Robinson has followed her to the front room and now stands behind her, close enough to put his arms around her and hold her.

"We will," he says softly, "we will."

She doesn't need to know his plan.

100

Robinson closes the laptop once more. It's time to take action now. And that is going to mean getting into the doctor's study. Without being seen or caught.

There's always a gap in security, somewhere, whatever the system. He just needs to figure out where.

He closes his eyes and thinks back to his last visit to the house. He remembers the lounge, Joane on the sofa. The windows, all with magnetic contact alarms, the same as in his house. Not a surprise given both houses were built by the same developer. What matters most though, is that he can't recall seeing any infrared motion detector alarms; no little red lights blinking from a small white detector in the corners of the room when he was moving around.

So there's a weakness. And he can exploit that. Not in daylight hours. It'll have to be at night. He wants to just get over there tonight but he needs to prepare more.

First, he has to decide when exactly to go. After midnight, maybe two or three in the morning, that time when it is the lowest point in the body's circadian rhythms. Except these rhythms vary from person to person. Some body clocks run on a longer cycle than others. He just has to hope that Samza's body is wired the right way.

With a bit of luck, Robinson will be able to get in and out without being caught. Which makes him think about the need to be careful, to make certain that he leaves nothing that might identify him. The doctor has friends in the police force, and Robinson doesn't want to be at the sharp end of an investigation. His pulse is increasing as he thinks about what he is about to do, knowing the fear won't go until he's done it.

Then he makes the decision

There's no point waiting.

He'll go tonight.

101

The voice is familiar. It belongs to the driver of the Lexus.

"You need to pay me."

"But I don't have the money right now," replies Samza.

"What do you mean, you don't have the money? You told me it would be ready."

Samza knew this call would be coming.

"I know," he says, "but I didn't know the bank would stop me taking the money out."

"That's not my problem."

"I will pay you in no more than seven days. I guarantee it."

"Well now, *that* is your problem, right there."

"Why?"

"You'll have to pay me more."

"Why?"

"You told me it was an emergency. You told me to make it an accident. And you needed it straightaway. I obliged. You haven't. So if you don't want to be signing your own death certificate, you'll pay me what you owe, plus another five grand inconvenience fee, within 24 hours."

"I can't."

"Then get your pen out."

"Look, what about the day after tomorrow. I just need the time to get the money moved and to get the cash out. You know how difficult cash is nowadays. Unless you want bitcoin?"

"Fuck off! Do I sound like a fucking computer? I want cash. 48 hours, no more. I'll ring with instructions for delivery."

The caller disconnects and the doctor puts the phone down. His hand is shaking as he lets the device fall to the desk. He doesn't have the money and he'll need to find a solution.

And soon.

102

The bedside clock clicks over to 2.49 am. He knows because he has been watching it for 33 minutes now, each change of number bringing him closer.

Robinson listens once more to Jo's breathing. She is deep in sleep. He slides out of the covers and slips into Chloe's room to get dressed in the dark clothing he'd placed there a few hours earlier. Stealing downstairs, he picks up his keys, puts on a dark anorak and opens the door to the garage.

He picks up the torch from the shelf and shines it on the shelving that runs along one wall, lighting upon a small handyman's bag. He picks it up and checks it contains everything he'll need, then lifts the garage door slowly, wincing as he hears the squeak of metal rollers. Once there is a suitable gap, he drops underneath the door and out to the front of his house.

There are no lights on in any of the houses nearby and the streetlights have gone off now. Making his way to the roadway he smells the moisture in the air and knows it's going to rain. Fuck. He should have checked, although even if he had, he knows he would still want to try tonight.

As he reaches the front of Samza's driveway, a flash of white and brown shoots past him, sending his heart racing and stopping him in his tracks. But it's only a fox. He closes his eyes and takes a deep breath as he tries to regain control of his pulse rate. This kind of thing is definitely not what he is used to. But he has to continue now. If he turns and gives up, then he might very well not return on another night.

One more deep breath. A check of the angle of view of the CCTV camera at the front, and he's off, crossing the garden past the corner of the house and on to the edge that demarcates the property and the five-foot-high fence that separates front from back garden. He clambers painfully over the wooden fence and, with a thud that knocks the breath out of him, drops down to the grass beyond, hearing his anorak rip in the process. Ignoring the damage, he listens carefully, his eyes scanning the area in front of him for any sign he's been noticed. All is silent.

Now comes the tricky part. Moving over to the wall of the house, he drops below the small side window and opens his bag, pulling out gaffer tape and a diamond glass cutter. He scores two deep, vertical lines in the glass, set as far apart as possible and then tears off two long strips of gaffer tape, placing them horizontally across the middle section of the window and pressing firmly to ensure a good grip. The glass cutter squeaks as Robinson slides it across the horizontal at the top and bottom of the window, replaces both cutter and tape in the bag and then uses the side of his gloved fist to knock out the rectangle of glass. The glass cracks easily and he uses the tape to pull it back out of the window and stores the glass to the side, taking the tape off and storing it in the bag.

He puts his head inside, tilting it as he listens intently until he is certain there is no one moving in the house. Placing the bag in first, he pulls himself through the window and stops to check for any sign of a movement detector, even as he tells himself that if there were one it would certainly have gone off by now. His pulse only slows when he is certain there is no detector and there is no sign of having been heard.

He makes his way through the living room and into the study at the back, pausing by the stairs to listen once more. Still nothing.

There is a soft brushing of the carpet as he carefully pushes the door of the study. Then he stops.

A bright light shines directly in his face.

103

His heart tightens sharply and the pupils of his eyes contract instantly. Instinctively, he turns to face away from the source and abruptly the light disappears.

He turns back round slowly and the light reappears, strengthening as he turns. Then he understands; there is a photo frame reflecting the light from his torch.

He lets out a long slow breath and turns his head around the room, picking out a desk resting against the opposite wall, with a computer and monitor resting on the surface of the desk. Above the monitor are a number of largely empty shelves, built for books and files, only a few files and one or two books scattered across them either side of a large wooden Buddha figure. To the side of the Buddha are several photos all put together in some kind of framed collage. He peers more closely at it. The photos are all of two young people, a boy and a girl, pulling silly faces in a photo booth were mixed up with more artistic photographs- a perfectly focussed shot of her face, a close-up of a single clear eye, a shot of two lips pursed for a kiss and a piece of paper on which were the marks of a lipstick kiss. It is more like a shrine than a piece of art. Robinson wasn't sure who the girl is but the boy is a much slimmer and younger version of Samza. It sparks the thought that there is no other sign of an intimate relationship or a relative anywhere in the house. Unusual perhaps but Robinson recognises it doesn't mean a great deal in itself.

He puts the frame back and spends a moment trying to remember exactly how the frame had been positioned. He should have taken a photograph on his phone before moving it. It's too late now for the frame but a photo of the desk space seems like a good idea.

Moments later, his hands are shaking as he settles himself into the chair in front of the desk at the far wall. A computer screen and laptop are the only items on the surface, both appear turned off. His eyes close and he takes ten deep breaths, exhaling slowly as he tries to slow his pulse and regain control of his hands.

The therapy works and he pulls the nitrile gloves tighter on his hands, wriggling his fingers to get the best fit. He turns the torch off and puts his hands on the laptop, taking one more breath before opening it up and recoiling slightly as the screen springs to life.

The machine asks for a password. Of course it does. He knew it would and he knows that there is no way he can guess at this. He could just take the machine away and look later; a hell of a lot easier but if he does then Samza will know it has gone. And his crime would go from breaking and entering to theft. He's not ready to give up now though, because for most people, passwords are a nuisance. And the longer they get, the more complex the word, the more people need to write it down. And the irony of all this is that the safest place is not in a password manager or file in the computer, which can be hacked by virtue of being in digital form, but by being written down somewhere. Somewhere safe. This prevents remote hacking. Remote being the operative word. And there is no point writing it down and storing it anywhere other than close to the PC. Which means it'll be here somewhere.

All he needs to do is find the password.

104

Opening the top drawer of the desk reveals a selection of pens and post-its but no passwords. He flicks through the post-its. The top one is just a list of things to do; 'book airline ticket, pay Pitbull, talk to Dan re fees' and the rest are blank. He throws the pad back into the drawer and checks the rest of the papers. Nothing of any interest- an old newspaper clipping about a car accident, four US dollar bills, some utility bills and a credit card statement which is full of day-to-day charges such as petrol, food and such like. Nothing of any interest until he see a torn off piece of paper. It reads 'Take Care of MR.'

He wonders who MR is. And for some reason, Robinson doubts take care of means caring for him medically.

His thoughts are interrupted by a groan coming from upstairs, a groan immediately followed by the thud of footsteps moving around above him. Shit. He shuts the drawer, clicks off the monitor and pushes the laptop lid down. He lifts himself up from the chair as a sense of panic steals over him. He does not want to be caught and debates leaving immediately but before he can decide, the footsteps above stop moving and he hears a stream of water splashing upstairs.

Relief sweeps over him. He waits until the noise stops, the toilet flushes and the footsteps return. But there is something wrong. The feet are still moving but not back in the direction they came from; they are heading down the stairs. Fuck.

Robinson steps back behind the study door just as a light goes on in the hallway, throwing him into dark shadow, brightly illuminating the floor of the study and highlighting the bag in the middle of the study floor. There's no time to lose and he frantically steps forward, grabs the bag and steps back behind the door, clutching the bag to his chest as the doctor passes the doorway and heads into the kitchen.

Barely daring to breathe, Robinson stays fixed in place as he hears the sound of a tap and a glass and senses more than hears the man returning. The gap in the door jamb provides a clear view of a dishevelled doctor in wide-check pyjama bottoms and grey T-shirt stopping in the doorway of the study. The blood is pounding in Robinson's head as he lifts the bag up to shoulder height, ready to swing it hard round in the doctor's face the second he steps into the room.

The study light is switched on, momentarily blinding him and his grip tightens on the bag, adrenaline rushing through his veins as muscles twitch, waiting for a split-second while his brain tries to pick the precise moment to unleash the blow.

Then the light goes off and the doctor carries on walking, back up the stairs and across the landing to his bedroom.

Robinson slumps back against the wall, his shaking legs giving way as he slides down the wall. It's ten minutes before he moves, hoping that ten minutes is enough time for the doctor to have fallen asleep. It's time. Robinson hauls himself up to his feet and settles down once more. He clicks his head torch on and searches the second and third drawers, where he finds a small, black, hardbacked notebook. He flicks through the pages and finds it on the back page. A single word that is obviously a password.

He keys it in and the laptop comes to life. It's a familiar format but he can see some icons on the dock that are new to him. He mangles the words of a song as he tells himself, 'One step at a time, sweet Jesus, one step at a time'.

Start with the familiar stuff.

105

He clicks on the Excel icon. And his eyes open wide. The file list is fascinating reading in itself: 'Undertaker'. 'Insurance'. 'Genome'. 'Winslaw'. 'Consultations'.

Opening up 'Consultations', he finds a record of what looks like fees received for each discussion. Frustratingly, there is only a code for each consultation, the first being AKNMX, a code which he cannot fathom. He tries to move the letters along the alphabet, starting with 2 spaces (A becomes C, K becomes M and so on) and this produces CMPOZ. He tries moving along three and then four (both up and down the alphabet) but this produces nothing intelligible. There must be a look up table somewhere.

Robinson scours the index and finds nothing. He checks recent history and once again, no sign of a translation table. Shit. Might as well have a look at the other files instead. So he opens up the one marked 'Insurance'.

Or rather he tries to but a dialogue box appears asking for a password. The first password doesn't work. And it's the same for all the other files.

Outside the window the first sign of light is creeping in. He'll have to leave soon without any answers. For a moment he considers taking the laptop, but it's attached to some kind of security lock. With this much security, the man is clearly hiding things.

Robinson decides to take another look at the black notebook. A lot of scrawly handwriting that could be anything. He can make out some words but much of it seems to be related to medical terms and conditions, so even if it was readable, Robinson doubts he'd be able to understand it. He turns to the remaining desk drawers, his search becoming increasingly frantic as he flips through papers, bills and medical journals, finding nothing relevant. There *has* to be something that will decrypt the code somewhere but whatever it is, he doesn't think it's in the desk.

There is one thing that might be useful though. He pulls out a USB stick and connects it to the computer, planning to copy the files onto the USB and take that away. Except the machine won't let him. It needs a password once more and the one that opened the machine doesn't work here either. Fuck. Then he has an idea.

He can photograph the consultations file and the list of excel and word files; after all, the file names are visible in each programme even if he cannot get into them individually.

At least then he'll have some information. And maybe there'll be a way to decrypt the entries later.

It takes a few minutes to scroll down and photograph that file and the list of files.

All the time he's photographing, he is looking at the file names and trying to work out what they mean. He blinks and shakes his head to fight the fatigue that is setting in now. It's been a long night and he needs to get out. He starts to close down the programmes and is pressing the keypad at the very instant that he sees a file marked J. Stevens. For a moment it doesn't register, but then the connection is made; Stevens was Joanne's maiden name. Torn between the desire to check it out and the need to leave, his mind is made up by the sound of a series of beeps from upstairs. There's no time.

Closing down the laptop and checking to see he's put everything back in its place, he gets up and make his way to the front room and the window. His heart is racing now as he hears footsteps upstairs and adrenaline surges through him.

His foot is up on the windowsill when he hears running water. The sound makes him pause.

This is an opportunity.

106

If the doctor is having a shower, then there are a few minutes in which to make it look like the break in had a different purpose. A broken window and nothing stolen would make the doctor very suspicious.

Robinson turns back in the lounge and sees a small TV set. He quickly lifts it up, carrying it to the window and feeding it through the hole, dropping it down the wall and following it out of the house. Taking a deep breath of fresh air, he hoicks the handyman bag up his forearm, picks up the TV set and carries it over to the fence, dropping it over the top onto the grass on the other side, then climbing over himself.

In a matter of seconds, he has made it across the road and back into his garage. He pulls the doors closed and sits on the floor, resting against the door as he waits for his breathing and pulse to normalise. He knows he's not likely to be a suspect for stealing a TV but it's better to remove the evidence as soon as he can. The TV, his shoes, the gloves and his coat all go into the boot of his car and he heads indoors, to clean up, shower, dress and prepare for work.

Upstairs Joanne is awake. She felt him leave earlier and has been fitfully dozing while she waited for his to come back to bed.

And now he's back. She checks the clock and only one question comes to her.

What the hell is he up to?

107

"Are you mad?"

Joanne looks at her husband, her mouth open and eyebrows raised high, as she hears what he has been doing: "You broke in and stole his TV? Because you don't want him to know what you were looking for?"

She takes her hands from her hips and picks up the cigarette packet, her questions hanging heavy in the air as she lights up another cigarette and takes a deep drag.

"You think," she goes on, smoke pouring from her nostrils, "that because he has some standard security on his computer, he is hiding secrets. And because you think I was at his house, you think it has something to do with me and so you didn't tell me what kind of lunacy you were planning? God help me. It's enough to drive me to suicide."

"You've already tried that," says Robinson, the words escaping before his brain engages, drawing a sharp glance.

"Er, I know?"

"I'm sorry, that was unfair. It's just that I know there is something very wrong over there. That man is not to be trusted."

"What do you mean he's not to be trusted? If it wasn't for him, I might not be here now."

"That's not strictly true, you know. While you were sleeping at his house, he told me that the wounds weren't deep enough to kill you but," he adds hastily raising his hands, "it is understandable that you thought they might, and I know why you did it."

"Even if that were true and I wasn't going to die, he did try to save our daughter, didn't he? The man tries to keep her alive in her last moments on earth. How can that possibly make him untrustworthy?"

"I don't know," says Robinson, shaking his head. "But there's something about the way he behaves. It's as if he knows me. And we still don't know why Chloe was in the road at that time, do we?" He pauses and then asks another question; this time making it clear he was looking for an answer. "Do you have any idea why she was interested in him?"

Joanne stubs her cigarette out in the ashtray in front of her, grinding it hard into the glass.

"She wasn't interested in him. I would have known."

"Well, I think she might have been. I 'm not sure what it is but when I get into that computer of his, then I'm sure I will be able to find out."

"Matt, I don't think you should be going through his stuff in the first place. And whatever he has on his computer is none of your business, is it?"

"I can't just leave it."

"Why not? What's he done to you?"

Robinson looks down and rubs the back of his neck while he thinks about his response, sighing as he decides to explain.

"I know that his activities are tied up with Chloe's death somehow."

108

The doorbell rings.

Samza looks at the monitor, wondering what the hell she wants now.

Outside Joanne Robinson is standing close to the door, keeping her face turned away from the road as she waits. Seconds later, she stumbles through the door as he opens it and she strides into the living room. He follows her into the room, inviting her to sit on the sofa while he takes a seat on a worn leather armchair.

"This is unexpected but, of course, very welcome. How are you, Joanne?" he asks. "Are you feeling better?"

"I'm fine thanks but what's happened?"

"Eh?"

"The glass company van that was outside."

"So reassuring to know that neighbourhood watch only seems to kick into action after the event," he replied sarcastically.

"What event?"

He tells her it was just a botched burglary.

"Did they take your computer?"

Samza's face breaks into a knowing smile: "No, they didn't. I still have your data."

"I want you to get rid of it."

"The computer?"

"No, the data."

"The data *you* asked me to get."

"Yes. Everything. I want you to delete everything."

"Now I don't think you understand what you're asking."

"I do. Just delete the data. How hard can it be?"

"I don't know that I can do that, you know. There are very strict rules that govern safekeeping of data and I could be in real trouble if I'm found to have broken them. It could cost me my job."

"That didn't seem to worry you before, did it?"

"Yes, well it does now. There are audit teams scouring GP records, looking for misuse. And as you may well understand, the first sign of misuse is a series of data deletions. It's like picking up a red flag and waving it at them, telling them to investigate. And I DO NOT want to be investigated."

"I thought all this was done outside the NHS."

"Ah well, yes but no."

"What the fuck does that mean?"

"It means that although it was done privately, any kind of data audit can lead to discoveries that are best not made. You know, forgotten files and links that don't go anywhere. I have to tell you, it is very difficult to disguise deletion successfully. And that makes it expensive too."

"But you *have* to delete the data."

Samza frowns, using it to disguise the excitement he feels at her desperation.

This is another opportunity.

109

The doctor pauses, mulling over his options.

"Are you saying this is very important to you?"

"Yes. Of course it is. I don't want him ever to know. And he's getting suspicious already. I'm terrified he'll uncover things best left forgotten. Or deleted."

Samza is silent for a few moments, leaning forward in the chair as he stares at the floor. Then he shakes his head, gently and sorrowfully, and tells her that there really is nothing he can do. He tells her it's not something he can do, not when you consider the risks to him in doing it. He appreciates her perspective, he understands the need for secrecy and would like to protect her if he could, but under the circumstances he really can't see what he can do. The risks are the risks."

"But you promised me that it would always be secret."

"It is secret,' he confirms, "unless of course, someone finds it."

"That's why I want it deleted."

Samza takes a slow breath and tilts his head: "Un-less, of course, you can see your way to helping me with the costs of getting rid of the data and all traces of the deletion."

Joanne's eyes narrow as she assesses where this is going.

"How much?"

"It's really difficult to erase traces of the data deletion. I'll have to pay other people. And they pay people. None of this comes cheap. But if you want absolute discretion, it's a small price to pay."

"How much?"

"It's thousands, I'm afraid."

"How much?"

"I can get it all done for five thousand and I can delete the all the data on my computer now. You can watch while I do it and I will ensure the rest of the deletion, including on other people's records, is done within 24 hours."

"All of it? Every last bit?"

"Every last bit and byte."

"Okay. I'll get the money."

"Cash."

"I don't have it here now, do I?"

"I'll be in touch."

After she goes Samza smile turns to a frown.

Perhaps he should have asked for more.

110

Joanne leaves his house and walks slowly back to hers.

She doesn't really trust him. He just seemed too eager to charge her to delete the information. But on the other hand, she tells herself, he has kept everything confidential up to now. He hasn't said a word to her husband about any of it, despite having made quite a strong argument at the time that she ought to tell her husband, as if she had needed any more guilt heaped on her. Maybe it'll be okay. Maybe he'll stay silent. Maybe.

Whatever happens, it would be better if the doctor were not around. She can maybe get the data deleted but she won't be able to eliminate the threat from a doctor who knows. While ever he knows, she will be at risk. So something must be done. At some point.

She is back indoors now, making a cup of tea and standing at the kitchen sink while she thinks through the alternatives. Despite all she has tried, she still knows it would destroy her husband if he were to find out. It would make the burden of loss and grief he had to bear ten times worse. How could he mourn a daughter that he loved but hadn't been his?

It would end the marriage and for what benefit? So that the biological father could hate her too?

There is nothing more to be said. She just can't risk her husband ever finding out.

Now she needs to make sure he can't.

111

Joanne doesn't hear the front door opening and closing, nor does she sense the change in atmosphere with the rush of fresh air. She is still lost when Robinson interrupts her thoughts:

"What on earth is the matter? You look as though something horrible has just happened. What is it?"

With rapid blinking and a shake of the head, she comes back to the present.

"No," she says, "nothing has just happened. Nothing at all."

She knows he doesn't really believe her. But the unspoken challenge hangs in the air, the questions left unsaid as she walks past him, squeezing his arm as she passes and goes upstairs.

She knows too, that her parting words are not a surprise to him; the message has been the same for weeks now.

"I just need some time alone."

Robinson says nothing, just looks at her, dismayed as the pattern continues. He watches her turn and walk off, hearing her climb the stairs as he waits for something different. He waits in vain.

For a full minute he stands there, his face tilted slightly as he tries to understand what he is doing wrong; tries to figure out what he has to do to break this cycle of distance and disconnection. His shoulders drop and his head shakes from side to side as he decides there is no answer.

Unless. Unless and until he finds the truth.

Maybe then her mind will be set at ease.

112

Lying upstairs, she can hear him clunking around in the kitchen., She hears him clearing up, the domestic sounds of crockery and cutlery rising up in timeless ritual, the crumpling sound of the dishwasher door being shut, the clink of glasses and the slight bang of one particular cupboard door; the one which has been most used, the one that has needed repairing for years and the one that contains the whisky. She can picture him leaving the now clean kitchen and settling down in front of the television, flicking through channels until he finds some kind of sport that he can stare at. It's familiar, safe, a conduit to a past of routine family life, comforting and heartbreaking in equal measure.

She knows he will be downstairs for hours now. The volume on the TV is low and barely audible. She hates the fact that he watches this stuff without really being able to hear any commentary, but she loves him for it too. It is a habit that started when Chloe was a baby and demanded a silence in the house if she was to go to sleep in the evenings. He had simply accepted that it was what was needed and had gotten used to watching everything in near silence.

They have been arguing endlessly recently. Anything and everything displeasing the one or the other, a displacement of the frustration and helplessness that they were enduring at the same time but separately. He has been seeing more of his old friend Robin, driving out to see him and being brought back by taxi once a week for the last month, seeking solace in the bottle and in a life that didn't remind him of Chloe.

She takes comfort in the simple fact that neither Robin or her husband know the truth, that this unspoken lie can protect and soothe. Until it is exposed that is and then the acid of reality will do its work.

She turns over in bed once more, her mind unable to settle, her thoughts racing on. There is no simple answer. She can tell him and lose him. Or she can keep paying Samza until the money runs out. And then what? She'd have to tell him. Or worse, she might have to get involved with the doctor and that wouldn't end well.

She has already lost Chloe and though they have had difficult times over the years, she knows their marriage is as good as anyone else's. He's not perfect but she doesn't deserve any better, that's for sure.

And more than that, she can't bear to be alone right now, even with the guilt of certain knowledge. It was easier when she didn't know. She could deceive herself and she could leave it open for him on the basis that there was no proof. But now that she has her answer, she realises that, deep down, she has always known.

It's the doctor though that is stopping her sleeping. She knows he cannot be trusted. She knows there will be no peace while he knows the secret, let alone while he can prove it. She needs to find a way to make absolutely certain that he never says anything.

She doesn't want to go down that road though. Not if she can help it. Maybe she'll have a better answer in the morning.

She rolls onto her back and sighs, trying to banish these thoughts. She starts to tense then relax different muscle groups, imagining warm sunshine washing over her as she clears her mind and relaxes.

The answer, when it comes, is surprisingly easy. The approach needs thinking through, but she instinctively knows it'll work.

Better yet, it will please her husband, allow her to shift doubt and guilt onto Samza, and it will bring her worries to an end.

113

The door opens and Samza stands there in his dressing gown, an arrogant look on his face.

"So are you coming in?" he asks, "I hope you don't mind, I'm not yet dressed."

His tone that makes clear he couldn't care less whether she minded or not, adding "Not that it won't be something you haven't seen before anyway" and walking back to the kitchen and lifting the kettle.

Joanne doesn't understand the point he's making but chooses to let it go, following him back to the kitchen.

"So have you brought the money?" he asks.

"Yes I have. But I want proof of deletion."

She has no idea how she can get that but she needed to say something that sounded plausible. It seems to work as Samza turns from the kettle and nods.

"I'm glad you came to your senses."

She picks up her handbag and pulls out a scarf which she places to one side, takes her phone out and appears to turn it off before placing it on her knee, then she pulls out several bundles of £50 pound notes. Then some more, piling the money up on the floor.

"There," she says, "£5,000. Now let me see the data disappear. Permanently. And no more blackmail. Of any kind."

"Oh, don't worry. The data will all go," he says. "Every last bit and byte. And you'll never need to come back again. And for the record, let me be really clear. I haven't blackmailed you. at all. It is not a personal thing. Just a business transaction in which I shall carry out your instructions for a fee. Simple as that."

Joanne puts the scarf back in her bag, lifts the phone and the bag and stands up.

"It might have been business for you, but it was personal for me. My DNA, my data and you refused to destroy it without payment? How can that not be personal?"

Samza stands up, leaning down to pick up the money and checking it is all there, then turns to face her, flaunting the looseness of his robe.

"I didn't refuse to destroy it, by the way." He pauses and looks at her. "And talking of personal," he adds fingering the money, "I could give you some of this back, if you want?? In exchange for a little personal time? After all, you have done it before, haven't you?"

"That was a lifetime ago. After this, our business is finished. Completely. As will you be, if you try this anymore."

Samza frowns.

"What the hell are you talking about?"

"I've been streaming this encounter to a private account and it will be released if you don't delete everything. Properly."

Samza's eyes narrow and his lips tightened.

"Give me the phone."

"No. There's no point anyway, the video is saved in the cloud. So even if you get the phone, you can't delete it."

Joanne can see he's going to hit her. She turns her face as his hand lifts, trying to protect her phone and her head.

114

Her eyes flicker open. He is standing in the same place and his right hand is resting on top of the money. He smiles, a false smile that oozes menace.

"Let's see about that, shall we? Anyhow, why don't we deal with your data first?"

"That *is* the whole point," she says.

The doctor's smile broadens.

"Would you like to go on through to the study, so we can do this?"

She follows him down to the study, aware he'll be scheming but whatever he is thinking, she has the evidence. And she wants the data gone.

She watches as he fires up his computer, pulls a tatty sudoku book from the shelves and flicks through it until he finds a page with paper inside- a paper that has been glued onto the page but which she can see has a number of names on it, including hers. His fingers trace the line and then he writes down a couple of numbers. Then asks her to turn round while he searches for her files, promising that when he has them on screen, he'll show her the deletion.

"You can look now."

She watches as him as dialog boxes appear and disappear, and documents are deleted, the trash is deleted and Samza turns to her as he gets up from the chair and makes room for her to sit at the machine. He opens up a search box and invites her to search for those names in the database. She keys them in and smiles as she reads 'No records found.'

Samza puts his hand on her shoulder and looks directly into her face:

"Okay. Now, I've done this because I want you to know I'm sincere. The deletions can still be tracked by the authorities and I shall ensure that steps are taken to eliminate all traces. That, my dear, is why I needed the money to finish the job- and it's as much for my benefit as yours, so you can rest assured full deletion takes place."

Samza shows her to the door and waves to her as she leaves, smiling at her, looking for all the world as if he's just saying goodbye to a friend. She doesn't turn around.

Once she has left, the smile clears and Samza goes back to his computer and inserts a small thumb drive. Seconds later the deleted records have been restored.

You never know when they might come in handy again, he tells himself.

115

Joanne is standing by the window in the front room as Robinson pulls up to the driveway, watching him as he opens the car door, nods and heads to the house. She hears the key enter the lock, the click and shift in atmosphere as the door is pushed open. She waits while he hangs his coat up, still staring out of the window as he comes in.

"Hi hun," he says, "are you alright?"

She sighs.

"No. We need to talk."

Robinson is half-expecting it. He could sense it in the atmosphere when he walked in. She is going to have a go at him. He sits down.

Joanne walks over to the sofa, flicking ash from her cigarette into the ashtray while she tries to formulate the words.

"I have to tell you something that's been worrying me."

"Go on then."

"It's complicated. It's about the photo, the one of me by his door."

"So it *is* you?"

"Yes."

Robinson feels his heart rate rising as he waits to hear the confession, waits for an explanation.

There is silence as she mulls her next words but he can't wait.

"Why didn't you say that in the first place? Why didn't you tell me?" he asks.

She shrugs, her eyes closing briefly.

Robinson wants to know more.

"If you won't say why you didn't own up in the first place, then what the hell were you doing there?"

Joanne can feel her cheeks burning while he stares at her, a tension rising between them as she searches for a reply that will be convincing. But he's seen the burning cheeks.

"You're blushing. Are you having an affair with him? Is that why you were there?"

"Good God no. Of course not."

"So why was Chloe photographing you? Why was she watching you?"

"She wasn't watching me, per se, she was watching him. She told me she had heard a rumour that the doctor was dealing drugs and she wanted to find out. I was trying to help her, hence the visits to his place and the photo of me there."

"So why didn't you tell me?"

"The state you were in, it wouldn't have been a good idea."

"What do you mean?"

"Well, if you were to have thought she was investigating him, or that he was dealing drugs, then you would have even more reason to blame him for her death."

"That ties in with her phone and his gaslighting me with it."

Through narrowed eyes Joanne lights another cigarette from the butt of the old one, She stubs out the old one, crushing the remains repeatedly as she speaks:

"I'm beginning to wonder if you might be right about him being odd though."

"Welcome to the club."

"It's just that I have been thinking about the code thing you told me about and I think I know where he keeps it."

"So how, exactly, could you know that?"

116

Joanne knows she is committed now. And she needs to maintain a coherent narrative to the story.

"Because I saw him use it the day I went in to see him, the day that Chloe took that photo. We'd agreed that I would go and check him out. I don't know why. It wasn't as if he'd be sitting there with a pile of drugs in front of him, weighing out the wraps. But Chloe wanted to know more about him and the house, so I agreed to go in for a chat. She was going to watch me and that's when she took the photo. I knew she was being overly dramatic, but sometimes it's just easier to give in, isn't it? You know how she is when she gets going."

Joanne gulps and draws a deep breath before she adds the word 'was'.

"Anyhow, we decided that I would go in on the pretext of just having a chat, you know, friendly neighbour, that kind of thing. He didn't believe me of course, but I told him I wanted to invite him to a dinner party I was putting together and wanted to see what dates might suit him."

She takes a drag, hesitating as she frames her words:

"I followed him into his study. He was looking at the screen and I was looking around his desk, trying not to be seen looking you know. But there was a booklet on his desk. Either a crossword or sudoku booklet. I couldn't be sure which."

"So?"

She went on to tell him about the paper glued in place, the two columns, the look of the words and letters.

"So?"

"I'm trying to tell you; it looked like a list of those codes you talked about after you broke in."

Robinson looks at her, trying to assess the information she was giving him. He doesn't doubt the booklet bit, that much is palpably true. What he doesn't believe is the dinner party excuse. Yet he knows that she will stick with it and there's nothing he can do to get her to shift. After all, they've been married for long enough to know.

"Well that might be handy, if I could get hold of his computer again."

"And that's the other thing I wanted to tell you", says Joanne, "he has had the glass replaced."

"So?"

"It means you can go in again, doesn't it?"

"Maybe just take the computer out this time? It means we can both check out the contents. Make sure we haven't missed anything."

"I'll see. Last time it looked like the laptop was alarmed."

Joanne isn't put off.

"Well try anyway."

117

This time the digital announcement board reads *Mr Robinson to Room 4.*

Robinson gets up, takes a squirt of hand sanitiser and heads down the hallway. He has to confront the man and this seems the safest place to do it.

He doesn't knock, just pushes the door open and walks in to see Samza typing. Without looking up the doctor speaks:

"Take a seat. Won't be too long."

A few moments later he lifts his head and his eyebrows rise.

"What can I do for you Mr Robinson?"

The response was not what he was expecting.

"How long have you been having an affair with my wife?"

"I beg your pardon?"

"You heard."

Samza's eyes narrow, his lips tighten and his chin rises as he considers his reply.

"Your wife was consulting me for advice, that is all. I was not having an affair."

"Really? What kind of advice did she want from you?"

"I can't say."

"You can but you won't."

Robinson stands up, puts his hands on the front of the doctor's desk and leans forward, jutting his chin forward to make his point:

"Well, what *can* you fucking say? And you'd better have something useful to say or you won't be speaking for quite some time."

Samza nods, holding his hand out with the palm upward, indicating that Robinson should sit down once more. He waits for the visitor to lift his hands off the desk and come to rest on the arms of the chair.

"Are you sure you want to hear this?" asks the doctor, knowing the question would only have one answer.

"Yes I am."

"Alright then. I'll just say it: Chloe isn't your daughter."

Robinson's response is immediate.

"You can fuck right off. I saw her. I was there when she was born."

"Yes," says Samza, "you probably were. But you weren't there when she was conceived, were you?"

"How the fuck would you know?"

"I'm her doctor."

"But why are you telling me this?"

Samza tips his head to one side and his expression softens along with his voice:

"Because you need to know. Because you deserve to know."

Robinson's face contorts as he tries to understand the implications of what he has been told. The daughter he mourned was not his. His wife had been unfaithful. His love had been built on a lie. And yet he had loved Chloe as much as any man ever loved a daughter and the pain he felt then and now was as real as if she were his.

Then reason begins to take hold. It simply can't be true. Samza is just messing with his head because he'd accused him of having an affair with his...the penny dropped.

Was Samza the father?

118

Robinson drops back into the chair behind him, trying desperately to find anything that didn't seem right when Chloe was conceived. And failing. He can't point to a single moment when she had ever known, let alone slept with the doctor back then.

"You don't believe me, do you?" asks Samza

"No, I don't. I don't know why you are pulling this stunt but no, I don't believe you."

"What if I could show you?"

"Show me what?"

"Proof that I have 'known'- Samza's first two fingers forming inverted commas mid-air as he said this- your wife?"

"I won't believe you."

The corners of Samza's mouth curl as he looked back at Robinson, holding his gaze, taking on the challenge in his eyes.

"She has two moles at the very top of her left thigh. One large and one small."

Instantly Robinson's eyes harden, a protective wall going up in his mind as his body prepares, his hands clenching, his legs tensing. He leans forward. And then softens. His eyes relax and he sits back in the chair, his head rolling from side to side as he begins to understand.

"Do you know, I nearly fell for that. I don't know why you said it because for a moment there, just for a moment, I was ready to kill you. But for the fact that you are a doctor, her doctor, and so you would probably know about the moles anyway."

The doctor smiles and looks straight at Robinson.

"You are right, I am playing with you."

Robinson breathes a sigh of relief, but it's a sigh that is unsatisfactory, an incomplete exhalation of the anxiety inside. The doctor's words have left an imprint, a mark that cannot be erased by a simple confession or a long sigh. They have taken hold and burrowed into his subconscious, even as Samza apologises for what he now calls teasing.

"You see, I think when you come in here falsely accusing me of having an affair with your wife, I am entitled to respond. And whilst I acknowledge I may have overstepped the mark and gone a bit far in my response, please hear me when I tell you I am sorry for causing you anxiety and for lying to you."

Robinson grunts. It's time to leave now.

He stands and looks down at the doctor: "You think you're so fucking clever, don't you? Think it's okay to say stuff like that?"

Samza pushes his chair back, crosses his leg and picks invisible fluff from his thigh.

"MISTER Robinson, I would simply advise you that if you come into MY surgery, making wild accusations, then I shall respond as I see fit. That said, as a doctor, my professional advice is that you sit down with your wife and talk things through, before it all gets out of hand. Let's just put this down to the stress of the situation, shall we?"

Robinson doesn't reply. He leaves, letting the door bang shut behind him.

The doctor smiles broadly and stands to look out of the window, watching as Robinson gets into his car and drives off, his wheels squealing as he leaves his parking space.

Samza turns back to the room and presses the buzzer for the next patient.

119

Alan is enjoying his new-found sense of freedom. From the moment he saw the bike, he knew he wanted it. It was a bike he had owned many years before and now was classified as a classic bike. The one he had seen was a fully restored, 1990 BMW r100rt with a tan saddle, white petrol tank and 20,000 miles on the clock. It isn't the fastest motorbike nor, necessarily, the coolest looking but he had wanted one when they first came out and that desire had stayed with him. So now, well into mid-life crisis territory, he had splashed out more than £10,000 to buy one. And he loves it. The way it handles, the unique noise that BMW engines make; the fact that it has plenty of power but not so much that he can't handle it...yes, he loves it.

And today the weather is fabulous, a crystal-clear sky, a warm sun and he is savouring every moment as he pulls down his visor, ready to pile on the power when he reaches the derestricted sign in a few hundred yards.

Up ahead the road is clear and he breaks into a wide grin as he twists the throttle back and feels the bike smoothly picking up speed. He looks down at the speedometer as it sweeps up, from 30 to 40 and now 50.

This bike is everything he wanted.

For now.

120

In his car, Robinson's mind is in turmoil. Did she really have an affair? He doubted it. But how can you ever be really sure? There was nothing that had made him worry in all their time together, and certainly not with Samza, but then some people don't know when partners have affairs, do they? If it had been eight years ago, that might have been possible because he remembers the two of them were struggling back then. But they'd worked it through and become settled and close ever since. But before Chloe was born? He shakes his head. It just seems inconceivable. But what motive would Samza have for lying? Saying it just to wind him up seems too much of a stretch. Unless the doctor is even more malevolent than he appears.

Robinson can feel the fear and anger inside him mixing in equal measure. What if she did? And how could she have had an affair? How could she let him bring up Chloe all the years as if she were his own and knowing that the girl's father was someone else?

Why would she have ever had reason to be anywhere near the doctor anyway? At the time Samza wasn't a friend of either of them and, as far as Robinson could remember, the man's name was never mentioned. So, though he cannot know for sure, it just doesn't seem credible that the doctor had an affair with Jo all those years ago. But there is something about the way the doctor spoke that is unsettling. It's true she does have the moles the doctor described but a doctor would know that. No, he's certain. The doctor isn't Chloe's father, even if it's possible someone else is.

So if it isn't Samza, then who is it?

121

Robinson is still thinking about who the lover might be as he starts the car and puts it into gear. He reaches the edge of the car park and looks out onto the road; knowing it will likely be clear of traffic, his foot stays off the brake as he glides out onto the main road, turns the steering wheel and then presses his foot to the accelerator.

Alan can see the nose of the car emerging at the same moment that his wrist twists and the smooth power of his 1200cc engine surges through the drive shaft and out to the back wheel, his body pulled back momentarily by the acceleration. The car should stop just as soon as the driver looks to his right and sees the bike fast approaching. Alan shifts his balance slightly, tipping the bike fractionally to the right in order to position the machine towards the centre of the road, just in case the man sees him late.

The closing distance is rapidly shrinking and Alan realises that the car is exiting quicker than he expects, the time between the first sign of a bumper and the front windows only a fraction of a second. Now he is much closer, and his eyes pick out the closed driver's window, a quick flash of a face as the driver focusses on the road to his left and fails to check traffic to his right.

In the split seconds remaining Alan knows he won't be able to swerve to avoid the car- it's pulling out too fast, he's too close and the switch in direction would cause the bike to fall, causing it to slide towards the car and trap his leg beneath the engine. Instinctively his hands grasp at both the clutch and the front brake and his right foot stamps on the rear brake. He feels the bike twitch and wriggle beneath him, momentum tipping him forwards as the brakes grip hard.

The man in the car turns his head and his eyes widen as he sees the bike careering towards him. Alan leans forwards on the handlebars, bracing for an impact.

Inexplicably the driver hits the brake and stops the car dead. Fighting to retain control of the bike, Alan can hear the squealing of his tyres.

In the final milliseconds, time slows, and he watches as the driver's eyes close and his head turns away from the approaching bike.

122

The front wheel hits the driver's door, driving the soft metal of the panel inwards, stopping the bike dead. Alan's grip on the handlebars is lost as his own weight takes him upwards, smashing his body into the edge of the roof, driving the hard metal edge into his belly, momentum causing his head to smack down hard on the roof of the car, leaving a large dent before Alan slides down the side of the car. Beneath him the back end of the bike slides forward, slamming into the side of the car, the lower edges of the wheels slipping under the car sills. A barely conscious Alan feels an excruciating stab of agony shoot through him as his leg is crushed and he falls back, twisting his body and tearing the ligaments in his shattered leg. His head bangs on the tarmac as his body comes to rest on the hot engine. Dimly he can feel the heat burning through his jacket and can smell petrol leaking from the tank beneath him.

A passer-by has run up to him and is lifting him, tugging hard at his body to try and free his broken leg. Alan's scream of pain is only partially obscured by the visor of his helmet, yet the pulling continues. He blacks out as he feels something give and his body is hauled away to the side of the pavement.

Slowly he is coming round. He can sense light and can hear a muffled voice asking if he is okay. He can feel fresh air on his face as the visor is lifted and the voice becomes marginally clearer. And then the pain of his leg hits him one more time. At least, he tells himself, I'm not paralysed. This is his last thought before sinking once more into the empty darkness of oblivion.

123

It's early afternoon and Joanne is sitting in the kitchen. On the table in front of her is a small plate on which lies a half-eaten sandwich whose crusts are beginning to curl up. Next to it is a partially drunk mug of tea, the tannin forming a hard line on the edge of the cold liquid. By the side of the cup is a glass ashtray, the edges overflowing with ash.

The front door slams and Robinson walks through to the sink, washing his hands before leaning in to give his wife a peck on the cheek, taking in the unfinished lunch as he does so.

"What did you do to your face?" asks Joanne, her hand lifting up to brush away his hair to get a better look.

Robinson gently touches her hand as he launches into his defence.

"*I* didn't do anything. Some nutty biker was going too fast and wasn't able to brake in time. So he's smashed into the car door and shattered the window. Some of the glass caught me that's all. I had to climb out of the passenger side. The car still drives fine though."

"Oh well that's alright then," she replies. "Funny though isn't it, how it's always someone else's fault?"

Robinson is too intent on his defence to pick up on the mood music.

"I just didn't see him until it was too late. He must have been going at a hell of a speed to get to me in the short time from me looking to me pulling out."

Joanne looks openly sceptical, setting off yet more protesting:

"Even the police said it looked as though he had been going too fast, to judge from the tyre marks on the road."

"You still didn't see him though, did you?"

"Not really," he admits, "but given how fast he was going, it's hardly surprising is it?"

Joanne briefly raises an eyebrow and then concentrates on lighting up a cigarette, taking a long first pull and lifting her face to blow out a stream of smoke. She picks a fragment of tobacco off her tongue and then looks directly at him. Robinson has seen this look before and knows he's going to be squirming soon.

"What were you doing at the surgery?" she asks in a light tone that belies the danger he is in.

"I just wanted to ask him something."

Jo's heart rate rises still further as she weighs up whether to ask the next question.

"What did you want to ask him?"

Robinson looks embarrassed.

"I was just trying to find out if you and he were…"

"Oh for God's sake! You ever known me all these years and I promise you I've been a faithful wife to you all these years. And if I were to look at a man it certainly wouldn't be an oddity like that man!"

"I know it's stupid. It's just that with the photo and everything."

"Forget about the photo and concentrate on getting that man's computer. That will be a far better use of your time, believe me."

"Perhaps you're right," he says, in that way that means I think you're wrong.

"I know I am. And hon, don't worry about the other stuff."

"I won't," he lies.

He knows there'll be time enough for that once he's dealt with Samza.

124

The back door opens with a squeak and Robinson stands on the doorstep, taking a deep breath as he contemplates the night ahead. The first time around had been exhausting. He's not a criminal and he doesn't enjoy the fear that goes with the risks of being caught. He can't figure out exactly what it is that scares him so. Being shouted out and told to fuck off is no big deal; being in a fight is something he would rather avoid but he's been in a few in his time, so he knows that bruises and bones heal. If he is caught and hauled off to the police station to be charged with something, he'll just plead the pressures and stress of the loss of his daughter and he's sure he'll avoid a custodial sentence. Assuming of course that he's not dealing with one of Samza's friends. Which makes him even more anxious as he thinks about it.

He senses more than hears Joanne step up to him as she reaches out, slipping her arms around his waist. He feels her cheek nuzzling into his neck as she pulls him closer and murmurs that he shouldn't worry. He's been in and out before, perfectly safely. He can do it again.

"It's just bloody stressful," Robinson replies, putting his hands on his wife's and squeezing gently. "I need to go up and get ready," he adds, turning to kiss her on the forehead before he goes back indoors to change. Joanne steps back into the kitchen and fills the kettle. She has been awake for several hours now while Robinson lay upstairs tossing and turning, failing to get any kind of peace, and then coming down to sit with her while they watched the clock turn towards the lowest point of the night. She will sit waiting for him to return once he's gone.

She has just finished making her tea when she hears him coming downstairs, dressed in black. He stands by the back door and puts his black trainers on, slips on a beanie and tugs a pair of nitrile gloves on. She lifts her cheek for a kiss and then he's gone, taking the small bag with him.

Without conscious though she rises and walks through the house to the front window, scanning for a shadowy figure soundlessly gliding across to the Doctor's house. A dark figure is moving along the edge of the hedges and then disappears from view. She pictures him climbing over the garden fence and settling down by the same window. There is nothing she can do here. No warning she can pass on. Even so, she feels the anxiety of having her husband going that close to the secrets that once were there. Provided, he tells herself, provide he gets in and out without being caught, then she can be sure Samza won't say anything.

If he's caught, then it will be a different story.

125

The putty is coming away easily. His fingers find the pins holding the glass in place and a pair of pliers makes short work of them.

The glass falls back into his hand and he carefully places it beside the wall where a new tub of putty is ready to be used to hide the repair. He won't be able to do it properly, tacking the glass into place, but with enough putty that's not going to be a problem. He puts his head into the room and listens carefully, his eyes scanning for any sign of additional security. It all looks much the same, albeit without a TV.

Two minutes later and he is in. A creak from above stops him in his tracks. He stands stock still, holding his breath, his heart pounding as he waits for the next sound.

There isn't one. It had simply been the sound of contraction as the house cools overnight. Feeling foolish, he exhales fully and makes his way past the staircase and back to the study, where he opens the door.

The computer is still there, the lid is closed and the monitor turned off, a red standby light staring out at him. He pushes the door back on its hinges, not quite closing it for fear of making a noise. Robinson clicks his head lamp on, lifts the laptop lid and turns to the shelves, searching for the booklet. He scans all the shelves and then looks again, mores slowly this time, more methodically but it doesn't change anything. There is no booklet visible anywhere.

Fuck.

This was always crazy. He thinks it might just be best if he forgets the whole thing now. He can just pack up, get out while he can and then it'll all be over.

Except he knows it won't be. He'll always wonder why he didn't check more, why he didn't have the courage to look. And wonder what he might have known. No, it's better to carry on. He takes a deep breath and once more searches the study, combing gently through the bookshelves, looking through the cupboards beneath the shelves, rummaging through the desk. Still nothing. He lifts up everything on the desk, looking underneath papers, lifting the laptop, even bending down to check under the cushion of the armchair in the corner. Nothing.

Frustrated, he straightens up and stops sharply. Something is out of place. His eyes have caught it but it hasn't fully registered. His eyes close as he tries to recall what flashed through his vision. A smile creeps across his face as he remembers. Dropping down to his knees he looks under the desk and sees it. A small corner of white-ish paper poking out from the back of the modesty board. He reaches in and pulls the corner, watching the rest of the pamphlet appear as he draws his hand out. This is it. It's a sudoku booklet and there is the page with the codes on. He sits back on the armchair and begins reading, ignoring the codes and looking directly at the names that follow them. And it's a list that would need to be kept secret. There is Winslaw, Anderson, Williams the Superintendent and several other names that he doesn't recognise. This time Joanne's maiden name is listed against a codeword. So there's more on her.

His stomach is churning as fear steals through his body and a real sense of dizziness hits him as he begins to digest the possibilities.

Once you open this up, you can't go back. He sits still for several long seconds, hesitating as he tries to decide the best course of action. He doesn't need the delay though.

He knows what he is going to do.

126

He navigates his way through to the files and the first one he looks at is for Joanne. There seem to be a number of notes against this file, each one dated. The first file showing is the latest, dated three weeks earlier. *'Results'.* He clicks on the file.

'Test results in. Discussed next steps. Joanne doesn't want anyone to know she has been in for the test. Opportunity. 10-50k'

Robinson frowns and slumps back into the chair, reading and re-reading the lines. What the hell test was she having? Why would she be seeing Dr Samza at his house and not the surgery? Maybe she isn't having an affair after all. Maybe it's a pregnancy test? She might still be able to have children. And if she is pregnant, who is the father?

Then he moves down the page and opens the file with Winslaw's name on it. This is more revealing. It looks like he is supplying goods. Against a series of dates are quantities of what are presumably drugs that have been sold. A lot of dates. A lot of amounts.

Whatever it is it looks to be lucrative and has been taking place for years. No wonder the policeman and the doctor seemed so friendly with each other. Robinson wants to look at the next sheet, the one for an insurance company. He clicks on the file name and hears a click that is louder than the last one. Then there's another one, this time louder, more solid.

Robinson holds still, his ears straining to hear more, trying to identify the sound that he fears. The 'clicks' of a spring turns into a creak and he knows the doctor is getting up. He shuts down the laptop and throws the codebook under the desk. He turns the head lamp off and his heart stops. Now there's a noise on the stairs. Shit. There's nowhere to go now. There's nowhere to hide. He needs to think. There must be a way out. His old exit route would take him through the hallway to the lounge and that's blocked and he knows he won't be able to get to the back door without being seen. Maybe if he could get out of the study? He leans over the desk and tries to twist the window handle. Fuck, it's locked. He can hear the steps are heavier now as the doctor gets closer. Robinson is scanning frantically for an exit, adrenaline coursing through his veins as he comes close to panic. A panic that explodes when he hears a voice shouting:

"GET THE FUCK OUT WHILE YOU STILL CAN!"

There are no options left now. He reaches across the desk and picks up the Buddha, feeling the heft of the wooden belly in his hands as he raises his arm and steps back behind the door. He peers through the gap in the door just as the hall lights are turned on.

Robinson sees the shadow in the hallway and then the doctor moves past him, unexpectedly heading for the kitchen. The fluorescent light flicks into life and seconds later he sees the man returning, his eyes looking at the open study door. The doctor's right hand is lifted up, a stainless-steel meat tenderiser glinting as he reaches the doorway and steps forward.

There is no time to think: Robinson shoves the door hard, feeling the thud as he catches the doctor broadside sending him hard in to the wall, dropping the tenderiser. Without waiting, Robinson brings the Buddha down hard and fast, waiting for the sickening crunch of bone breaking as it hits the doctor's head. But the doctor is too quick and his head slips to the side before the Buddha hits. But he's not quick enough to avoid it completely. The wooden ornament clips the side of his head, bouncing against the man's temple and then falling out of Robinson's hand to land on the floor, followed immediately by the now unconscious doctor who lands on his shoulder, collapsing his body into a twisted heap. A thin line of bright red blood runs silently from the side of his skull, pooling on the carpet, darkening as it settles in place.

127

Robinson stands still, contemplating what he has just done, repeating one word three times. Fuck. Fuck. Fuck.

His world has changed and now he is in even more danger. Murder is not what he intended but no-one will ever believe him; smashing a man's head with a solid wood ornament is never likely to end well. He kneels down beside the body as carefully as he can, trying to avoid any contact with it. He leans over the face, placing his ear close to the man's face. It's definitely there. The man is breathing. Shallow breaths for sure but he's alive.

Robinson rocks back on his heels, sitting down on the floor in the study as he tries to think what he's going to do next. He wants to read through the rest of the files on the computer but he's got other things to deal with now.

He needs to clean up before he goes anyway. Get rid of evidence he was there. That means putting it all back as he found it. It also means not stepping in or touching any of the blood. He steps over the body and goes into the kitchen, washing down the Buddha in the sink, scouring it hard with a scrubbing brush, rinsing repeatedly until he's convinced that he's removed any possible traces of blood from the edges. When he thinks it's clean, he tries to dry it off with a tea towel. The surface water has gone but there is a dark patch where water has penetrated. It'll dry, he decides.

He replaces the Buddha then opens up the laptop so that he can close all the dialog boxes and shut it down properly. The password book goes back in the drawer, he tucks the codebook behind the desk and picks up his bag, checking his pocket for his phone and steps over the body once more. He puts the study light on to get a good look around. It all looks good.

Leaving the lights on, he makes his way through the sitting room and climbs out of the window. All that's left is replacing the window. Even if it's put back badly, it'll still look like the originally recently replaced window. In any event it'll buy some time. Listening intently for any change in the night sounds, it takes him ten minutes to fix the glass back in place, using a hefty dose of putty. It's not well done but only the man from the glass company would know it wasn't his work. Looking around outside the window, he can see nothing left behind. Bending down he feels around the area to feel for anything that shouldn't be there. All is clear.

It takes less than a minute to get over the fence and make it back to the rear of his own house. He takes a deep breath and begins to plan. The clothes must be thrown away. Somewhere far away from the house. He will remove anything incriminating in the morning, when he's had time to think about what he might have left behind. The doctor won't be going anywhere anytime soon. All that's needed is to find a dustcart and his clothes, and any evidence will be gone. Especially the shoes, he tells himself.

He walks to the back door, taking off his shoes and gloves, before he goes in. Pushing open the back door, he jumps when he sees Joanne standing there, looking at him.

"What's happened? Did you get it?"

"No."

"So why do you look so terrified?"

"Christ Almighty, of course I look terrified. I'm not used to this, am I?"

"So what did you find out?"

"It's not what I found out. It's what we are going to do about it that matters."

128

Robinson pulls a bin bag out of a drawer and takes off his outer clothing, putting it all inside the bag and fetching his shoes and gloves from outside. He ties the bag up and tells her he's going to shower, suggesting she pour him a drink and then he'll be back down to talk to her. Reluctantly, Jo agrees, a rolling of her eyes disguising the tension she is feeling.

Five minutes later, he's sitting down with her, taking a full slug of whiskey before pouring some more and looking across at her. She takes a drag on a cigarette, exhales and looks back. Her eyebrows are raised.

"So?"

"I found details on some of the files. One of them seems to show him trading what I imagine to be drugs with DI Winslaw."

"Really? What sort of drugs?

"Obviously not the legal kind, not in the quantities that I saw."

"What about his doctor's oath?"

"He's not worried about that."

"God. What is a man who's a doctor doing selling drugs?"

"Making money," says Robinson flatly.

Joanne waits for him to continue. He doesn't.

"Are you sure you're okay?" she asks, her brow furrowing as she leans forward.

"Hon, you're beginning to worry me. What else happened?"

"Nothing. Nothing at all."

"Really?"

Robinson finishes off his whisky and put the glass slowly down on the table as he decided what to tell her.

"I found some other stuff,": he admits, "there were a number of files and one was something to do with an insurance company."

"What did it say?" says Joanne, struggling to keep relief out of her voice.

"Nothing. I couldn't finish. I heard noises above me, so I got out of there quickly. I had the window back and I was out of there before he had a chance to catch me."

Joanne watches as he stands up and put his glass in the sink. He stays looking out of the window for several minutes while Jo waits for him to turn round and then the two of them can go to bed and put this nightmare behind them. His shoulders drop as he exhales loudly and then slowly, wearily, turns to look at her.

She can feel an excruciatingly tight knot in her stomach, a knot that squeezes still tighter as she sees his face and hears his words.

"There's something else I have to tell you."

129

Joanne listens without interruption as he tells her how he had tried to hide and what happened when the doctor appeared with the weapon. He tells her that he thought the man was probably dead by now.

"He was barely breathing and he was bleeding from his skull."

"Head wounds always bleed heavily, everyone knows that. You've probably just knocked him out. Which won't be a bad thing because it might mean his memory isn't so good. Which won't hurt, either way."

"Maybe I should have phoned for an ambulance?"

"That would have been stupid, wouldn't it?" says Joanne. "If you'd phoned for an ambulance, they'd have known who it was. And if you've hurt him badly then you'd be in deeper shit."

"Maybe, but I hadn't intended to kill the man. I wanted out without being seen."

"For fuck's sake, It's too late for that. If he's badly enough injured for the police to investigate, don't you think they would make a connection between you going round before, being seen on CCTV. They will probably know someone was on his computer. There'll definitely be an exact time there. Although I suppose they might think it was him. And don't you think that there'll be some forensic evidence somewhere?"

"I don't think so. My clothing and footwear are all in the bag I'm going to get rid of today. So no, there won't be. Not from last night. And even if there were some, we've both been in his house legitimately before so there's no risk. "

Robinson pushes himself up and moves to sit at the table.

"So let's just sit tight. The one thing we can't do is act any different to normal; if we change out routines people might think it was something to do with me. As it is, he'll have no idea. So I'll dispose of the evidence tomorrow on the way to work; I'll find a bin lorry or just any bin not in front of a camera and then it'll be gone. There will be nothing to link us to the crime."

"Us? I didn't hit the man. You did!"

"Okay, but you're not going to say anything are you? I mean a wife can't testify against her husband, can she?"

"I don't know. I just worry something in there will link it to you or me and then if they find out we've covered it up…" her hands rise to her mouth and she holds them there, cutting off the thought before the

344

words are spoken, deciding instead to ask the question:

"Did you see anything in there that might point the finger at us?"

Robinson pauses while he thinks about his response, allowing Joanne to think he's searching his memory. There is, he decides, no point telling her now.

"No," he lies, pausing before he goes on, "Nothing at all."

Joanne doesn't believe him and pushes for more.

"So what else did you find, then?"

"I didn't get much time to search through but what I did find was that Winslaw is buying drugs from Samza and then, presumably, selling them. Which means we can't rely on Winslaw to investigate anything to do with Samza properly."

"So you're saying Winslaw is corrupt."

"Not just him. The superintendent Williams is also in there. Which means he had powerful friends. And I don't know where that leaves us."

130

Joanne is still awake. Robinson has gone to sleep, exhausted by the anxiety and fear of night but she is wide awake. Wondering what he actually saw and what he is hiding from her. She sighs heavily and throws back the covers as she gets up, giving up on the idea of sleep. Her dressing gown is hanging on the back of the door and as she walks around the bed, something catches her eye, something which registers as she reaches out to pick up the robe.

The lights are on in Samza's house. None upstairs but the downstairs lights are all on. A shot of fear snatches her breath from her as she panics about the break in. Did he leave anything behind? And worse, what might he have seen that he hasn't told her about. Samza appeared to have deleted all the computer records but she cannot know what else he had in his study somewhere, what else her husband might have seen.

She is still standing at the window when she sees the light pattern change. The upstairs lights come on and downstairs lights go off. Then the upstairs lights go out.

She snorts at the irony; at least she won't be a murderer's wife even if he is a married to a woman who caused her daughter's death.

She can't keep the secret for much longer.

She'll have to tell him.

And soon.

131

The next morning things seem clearer. There is only one sensible thing to do, Joanne tells herself. All the other choices lead to the same point eventually. So why prevaricate anymore? Just tell him and get it over and done with.

Perhaps he will understand. Perhaps he will realise that nothing in the last twenty years was unreal. It all happened; the feelings were still the same, the love was the same. Nothing he experienced is suddenly undone. Whatever misconception it was founded upon, their reality had been their reality. And the child was a separate human being not something two people owned.

And what if they had both known she wasn't his? What if she'd adopted it would have been the same, wouldn't it? Or would it have been worse because no part of the child would have been theirs?

But the issue, the real problem, is not knowing what to do. That much is now obvious; in fact, it has always been obvious. The problem is *how* to tell him. How can she find the words to start a discussion?

She had been trying out various combinations in her mind for years. "I have something really important to say." "I love you very much and there is something I have to say about the past." "I haven't told you everything about me." "Hon, we really need to talk about Chloe." "I haven't been honest with you and I really should have…" she has tried a thousand versions out in her head but there is no version that begins to work. Maybe she just needs to come out with it.

Just tell him as it is.

Soon.

132

It's a difficult conversation.

Made more difficult by Robinson's questions about her moles.

At first, she tries a small lie.

She tells him husband that Samza has been seeing her for a 'woman's thing' and that this explains how he knows. It's logical but Robinson just doesn't buy it.

"I know this matches with what he said but there's something wrong, Joanne. It doesn't fit. You would have told me if you'd had a medical problem and the way he was saying it, it was as if he knew it wasn't true and I wouldn't believe him. He's hiding something and I know you are too."

She's reluctant to say it but knows there is little choice.

"Okay, I'll tell you everything."

She tells him about Chloe, about the doubt that has always been there. She tells him that she had been with someone else, once, before they were married.

"I couldn't know for sure and she was almost certainly yours. With him, it was only once. And with you it was many more times, and different, and better and…"

'But why didn't you tell me?" complains Robinson, knowing the answer before she gives it.

"How could I? And after I didn't tell you immediately, then it just got harder. And harder. With every day that went by it faded into the past and once you saw Chloe and I could see how much you loved her, then I knew I couldn't tell you. And I never would have."

Now it all makes sense. It was a paternity test. Yet he has to know more.

"Why go to find out now?" he asks.

"Because I wanted to know. Because I wanted to know for sure, now that she is gone. And...," she reaches across the table to take his face in her hands, her palms holding his cheeks as she looks directly in her eyes, "and I so wanted it to be you."

Robinson knows. His face says so before he does.

"But it wasn't, was it?"

Her hands slip down his face and she wraps his hands in hers as she prepares him for the next sentence, choosing her words carefully to focus on the things he wants to hear.

"You were always her real father. Not biologically perhaps but you were the father who loved her and cared for her, the one she knew as her father, and loved you as only a daughter can, whatever the biology says."

"For fuck's sake, Joanne! For fuck's sake!"

She watches as anguish rips across his face, the shock of her betrayal cutting deep. Joanne wants to stop now, to leave it here. But she can't. Her next sentence will only sharpen the pain:

"There's something else too."

133

Robinson's face crumples. He doesn't want to know. But he can't let it go.

"What is it?"

"Samza's been blackmailing me. Wanted £5,000 to stop him telling you about the paternity tests."

"Did you?"

"Yes, I gave him the money. I didn't want him to tell you. I wanted to tell you myself."

"That's hardly true, is it? You've had years to tell me."

"You know what I mean."

He swallows and rubs his hands over his face, trying to clear space to think in the face of the revelations.

For a few moments she thinks she has managed the impossible, she has managed to come clean and leave the conversation at Samza's blackmail. She sees the tears in his eyes as he thinks about Chloe and she feels his hands move to return her grip. But his grip tightens and his face darkens as he squeezes her fingers and asks the question she is dreading.

"Who was the biological father then? "

She hesitates. One thing at a time, even though the pressure on her hands is increasingly painful. She pulls away as she replies:

"That doesn't matter, does it? What possible good can come of talking about that now?"

"I want to know whose fucking child I brought up."

"She was your girl, your daughter, whatever the genetics."

Robinson stands now, his breath strong and noisy as he leans forward on the table and demands an answer.

"Who. Was. It?"

She gives up and tells him, seeing the confusion in his face as he tries to take in the name. Then he bangs the table with both fists and turns to open the back door.

"Robin? Fucking Robin?"

These are the last words she hears before he leaves and slams the door behind him.

She breathes a sigh of relief. The secret is out and she no longer has to pretend. Maybe now they can begin to put Chloe's death behind them. Except for one thing.

She hasn't explained the moles.

134

The noise of the slammed door fades, leaving behind an empty silence. A heavy, oppressive vacuum that forms an emotional black hole pulling at her thoughts, sapping any hope she has left. After 45 years of being on earth, her life has amounted to just this. No daughter, a husband about to leave her for good and a near-forgotten past that has returned. She could live with that past, she tells herself, she could get through it, if there was at least hope.

Unthinkingly, she lights another cigarette, seeking the comfort of addiction satisfied, the familiar feeling of filter against lip. Is this all that is left to her? One cigarette after another and hours of sitting in silence, a quiet broken only by the clicking of the radiators heating up, a metronome for the pointless continuation of her life; or a measure of each moment waiting; waiting for the axe to fall?

Yet even as a deep fatigue washes over her, she knows she can't accept this. She needs to find a way out. Just sitting around isn't an answer. Nor is waiting for the doctor to do even more damage. Doing nothing is simply a living death. And she doesn't want that. Which means the next steps have to be taken. Tomorrow.

For now, she's going to sleep. Slowly she rises from her chair, takes a last, long drag on the cigarette then stubs it out half-heartedly, leaving a part still alight in the ashtray. It's safe but she really doesn't care if it isn't. Joanne walks out of the kitchen, leaving the lights on, in case. In case he comes back tonight.

The stairs are hard work, each step seeming steeper than the last and her feet drag all the way to the bedroom. She doesn't undress, just dropping to the bed and pulling the duvet round her. Eyes close and in seconds she is asleep.

135

The car slows, indicates left and draws up to the edge of the park. Robinson steps out, pulls on the jacket from the back of the car and clicks the door shut. It's quiet at this time of night but there are still pedestrians walking along the road, down by the junction with Regent's Park Road. He crosses the road and enters Primrose Hill Park by a side gate, walking up to the peak and sitting at one of the benches. Next to him a small group of twenty-somethings are chattering loudly about the view, alcohol in their systems inhibiting their ability to control the volume of their speech. He knows they'll go soon, and ten minutes later his patience is rewarded.

It is soon silent and his mind turns back to the issues that brought him here. He needs to think. Oddly, it's not the affair that bothers him. He had noticed an attraction between the two of them back then and had always suspected that something had happened once, a thought sparked by something his best man had said when they were waiting for her one day. And it wasn't so much the words he used, it was the tone he used, a sense of finality in the man's voice that meant what he now knows was what he thought but had always ignored. It was just easier to tell himself his best mate would never do that.

Strangely he feels a sense of relief at finally knowing the truth. The ghost of an affair has now been laid to rest, he decides. Perhaps it is a fitting end. The story could not have been completed while Chloe was still alive. It would have been too difficult. Now the pieces have fallen into place and perhaps they can all move on.

Except. Except that there is something still not right. Why does he still have the nagging sensation that he is missing something? Maybe he needs to ask the right kind of questions. Whatever they might be.

Looking out across London, from Canary Wharf to the Shard and on to the London Eye, Robinson is reminded of his irrelevance in the overall scheme of things. He is just one of 8 million humans in the city tonight. The thought reminds him of that fateful night when he had been working in the city and had chosen to take a risk. A risk that hadn't paid off.

136

Tonight the face appears. It has been lurking in the darker recesses of her mind. An image that has never quite been erased. She's only half asleep when it appears. At first, she sees his eyes, his dark eyes looking out from a young, barely formed face. She cannot remember the name he used- Alan? Andrew? Adam? But whatever it was, the face is definitely him. It is a younger face than today of course; thinner, no beard, floppy hair.

This isn't a dream though. It's a memory. And now the way he looked at her returns, the way he stood there, awkwardly looking up at her nakedness. She had been sure it had been the first time he'd been in front of a naked woman. It was the intensity with which he drank in every feature. She had felt her skin crawl as long seconds passed and he just looked without saying anything. She had asked him if he was alright and he had shushed her, his eyes roaming across her body. She couldn't help the way she brought her hands down to cover exposed body. That was when he had commented. Nothing about her discomfort or his excessive staring. All he said were a few words, words which now come back hauntingly, the cold, sharp steel of the certainty of here memory deepening her fear.

"I didn't know moles grew there."

"That's not the only thing we can get to grow down there," she had said, reaching her hand forward, in the hope that the encounter would be as brief as it was uncomfortable. Moments later, her hand and body had been all that was needed to bring the encounter to an end.

She remembers she had called herself Arabella.

137

One week later

The light from the screen fades quickly as the doctor clicks the machine off. He rubs his eyes in fatigue then lifts his glass and finishes the last of his whisky and contemplates another. It's late and he's tired but he knows he's had a good day. The drugs company have paid him for his information and agreed a rate for increasing the number of patients he puts on a particular drug. It'll mean switching a few patients across but it shouldn't be a problem. And he can soon make it quite lucrative. Better still, the company he is working with are investing in tax-free Nassau, in the Bahamas.

He's also having to fend off a threat closer to home too. The other doctors in the practice are talking about selling the practice to an American outfit and that would inevitably compromise his ability to act quite so freely. He recently leaked details of a once very famous celebrity's mental health issues to a friendly journalist in need of a good story, so now it's time for the favour to be repaid. He needs a story on 'keep your NHS British'.

And better yet, he has paid Pitbull his money. The man continued to deny he had been the one to beat Samza up at his home, but the doctor knows better and now the bill is paid, he thinks he can afford to relax a bit.

Perhaps he will have another whisky after all. He stands up and walks round to the kitchen, thinking about getting something savoury to go with it when there is a loud banging on his front door; the banging that says I won't go away until you answer. For a fleeting moment he wonders if it's the police. He can't think of anything that's made him more vulnerable than usual but it's never impossible for something to have gone wrong. He can't hear them shouting out though and if it were really urgent, they'd have broken the door down by now.

"ALRIGHT! I'M COMING!"

Peering through the spyhole, he can only see the back of a hoodie. Warily, he hooks the chain on the door. It may not be the strongest thing in the world but at least it'll give the impression of security; enough to warrant opening up.

"Oh for fuck's sake, what do you want?" he asks when he sees the visitor

"You."

Robinson takes a step back from the doorway and then shoves himself forward hard against the door, ripping the security chain from its screws and thrusting the door hard into the doctor's chest, driving him backwards into the house.

"What the fuck?"

Robinson stands close, his face inches from the doctor.

"We need to talk."

Samza wipes his nose to check for blood. His hand comes back clean.

"This is hardly talking now, is it?" he mutters, angrily pushing Robinson back and making steps towards the kitchen. "And shut the fucking door," he snarls over his shoulder.

Robinson closes the door and follows the doctor, standing by the doorway as Samza takes up position leaning against the counter, deliberately obscuring the view of a knife block behind him.

"So what do you want to talk about then?"

"I think you know."

Samza knows he will enjoy this search for the truth and decides to prolong the fun.

"No, I'm really sorry, I have absolutely no idea."

138

The tactic produces a response alright. Just not the one he wants.

Too late Samza realises he should have pretended to be thinking so that he can reach behind him for a weapon, without being seen. But he takes too long. Robinson has reached the whisky bottle on the kitchen table, grabbed it and is swinging it as Samza's right hand finally locks onto a knife. His left arm comes up in defence, trying to shield his head from the blow, followed by excruciating pain as the bottle shatters the radius and ulna bones in his arm, leaving his hand hanging loose from a place several inches above his wrist. His right hand pulls the knife out of the block, feeling the gratifying weight of it in his hand. Fighting the agony of his broken arm, he stabs out at Robinson who jumps back, pulling in his stomach as he tries to avoid the end of the knife now thrusting forward, penetrating his skin but not deep enough to do real damage.

Samza realises he is in trouble. He's pulled out the bread knife, good for slashing but not stabbing. Samza's left arm is dangling uselessly now, his only defence the slashing knife. And he knows it's not enough.

Frantically he slashes the weapon to one side, then back again, repeatedly, driving his assailant back to the kitchen doorway.

Robinson scans the room for another weapon and sees nothing in range; appliances are plugged in and there is nothing to throw, beyond a couple of books buried beneath a crumpled tea-towel. Samza smiles. He might win this yet.

The two men stand staring at each other, open-mouthed and breathing heavily as each waits for the other to make a move. Samza knows he needs to be closer but he's only going to get one chance and there's no room to manoeuvre in the hallway. So he steps back, dropping the knife a few inches, marginally reducing the threat, encouraging Robinson to believe he's about to capitulate.

"Look, we can do this differently, can't we?" he says, "you've broken my arm, surely that's enough? So whatever you have to say, just say it and then get out. Leave it here and it'll all be over."

"You think this is just about a broken arm? You have been blackmailing my wife you miserable fucker. Blackmailing her to stop me finding out that my daughter was biologically someone else's. I've lost my daughter and you drove my wife to attempt suicide. You are a reptilian piece of shit."

"And you are a stupid, ignorant fool. You still don't understand, do you? You still haven't put two and two together."

"What the fuck are you saying?"

"You know what your wife did when she was a student, don't you?"

The doctor pauses, enjoying the opportunity to watch the confusion and anger playing out across Robinson's face, then he continues: "You don't know, do you? You don't know that she was on the game. Making ends meet by making ends meet, you might say."

"That's a lie."

"Oh no it isn't. How do you think I really got to know about the moles? She was my first, by the way. Your wife gave me my first experience." Samza shivers with pleasure and then a sly smile creeps over his face: "God, I still remember it now. You never forget your first, do you?"

"I don't believe you. You're a lying little shit."

"Oh it's true. Ask her. See how she reacts. And by the way, I still think I overpaid."

"Fuck you," says Robinson stepping forward.

139

"Uh-Uh," says Samza, lifting a hand to halt Robinson. "You want to know the whole story, don't you? Don't you want to hear the truth? And beating me up won't help you do that."

"I don't want to hear another lie from your stinking mouth."

"What I have told you is true."

"Yeah well, we all have a past," says Robinson.

"I know. Only too well."

"What does that mean?"

His smashed arm is sending shots of fire into his nervous system, making him wince in agony, yet this is the conversation he wants to have. He wants Robinson to know the truth. Then he's going to finish him. But first, he's going to get his revenge.

"Oh. you'll know. It's your past."

"Well, why don't you tell me?"

"A train journey. Drinking. The girl?"

Robinson flinches. It was all a long time ago. But he hasn't forgotten.

"I have no idea what you are talking about."

"Oh you do," hissed Samza: "You do. You drove when you were drunk. You...you are responsible and you have only just begun to pay the price."

"I was charged by the police over that accident. And I've paid the price."

Samza is incredulous.

"Price? The same price as if you'd hit a deer? Her life held the same value as a fucking deer?"

"Look, that was a long time ago and it's got nothing to do with you."

"Is that what you think? Did you not read the newspapers at the time? Did you not know her name? Go on, say her name."

"I er I don't remember now. It was um, Anna??"

"It was Emma."

Robinson's face blanched as understanding dawns.

"It was Emma. You're right."

Samza took a deep breath to control both the pain and his anger, his teeth clenched as he sneers back:

"Why couldn't you remember? Didn't it matter?"

"Of course it mattered. It's just that... it's just that I never saw her so I suppose I couldn't remember her name."

"You never saw her? You never fucking saw her? That is the whole fucking point!"

"Look, I cannot change that. I wish I could, but I can't."

Samza's shoulders drop, seemingly in defeat. He turns to his right and puts the knife down on the counter. Slowly Robinson edges forward, his right hand outstretched.

"Look, I am truly sorry. I really am."

In one smooth movement, Samza snatches the knife up once more and whirls round, slashing at Robinson's hand. Robinson tries to pull back but he is too slow. The knife slices through the distal joint of his middle finger, taking the top off completely. Aghast, Robinson looks down at his hand, sees the blood pulsing from the open end of his finger, sees the end of his finger bounce on the floor beneath and roll away from him.

Samza laughs, a cruel mirthless laugh that scares his opponent:

"Nothing you say can bring her back. But you can pay a price."

140

Clutching his right hand in his left, fingers pointing upwards, Robinson suddenly realises the danger he is in.

"I've said I am sorry. I truly am. And killing me won't solve anything."

"Maybe not for you. But it will make me feel good."

Samza knows that Robinson is right. Killing him now, with no preparation, no planning, will be too risky. Too much evidence. Too many things to go wrong. But there is still taunting to be done. That's much less risky.

Robinson backs away, slowly, hoping the space will de-escalate the situation.

"You can move back but it won't change things, will it? It won't change the fact that your daughter was someone else's child. Or that your wife was unfaithful and betrayed you. Betrayed you every single day of Chloe's short life."

Robinson stops moving.

"She may have been unfaithful once, but Chloe was my daughter. I loved her as only a real father can. Her biological father is irrelevant."

"Oh but it isn't."

Robinson frowns, uncertain where this is going.

"He's the one who got you off, isn't he? The one who came up with the deer scheme?"

"Robin? That was his job."

"His job was to help you get away with killing a girl. Not just any girl but a very special girl. A girl who was at the beginning of her life and who was making someone else's life complete."

Robinson breathes in, his face rising as he takes in the implications.

"You mean she...she was..."

"Yes, she was my fiancée. Or she was about to be. And you killed her. You should have died too. In the fire."

"It was you? Fuck. The fire. How did you find...?"

"Oh I have been waiting for years. Waiting. Waiting to have the perfect moment to take my revenge. And now I've got it."

Robinson smiles and chuckles.

"Well, not exactly revenge, is it? I mean, quite frankly, I think you've wasted your time. You can try to drive a wedge between us, try to find something in my past or hers but it's pointless. We've talked about all of it. Which makes this all a bit pointless doesn't it?"

Samza is watching Robinson's face as he says all this. Waiting. Waiting for the man to stop gloating. Waiting for the real pleasure that is to come. But Robinson is still talking:

"Look, I am sorry for what happened to your girlfriend. I really am. But it's in the past and we both have to let it go now, however painful that may be. Maybe I should just leave now. His tone softens and he steps back into the hallway. Out of range. Using distance to lower the temperature further. "Maybe," he says, "we should both just get on with our lives as best we can."

"I can. But you will find it difficult. Because of what you are about to find out. You are going to find out who paid for your daughter to be killed. Killed in the same way as the love of my life died. Well," he sniggers, "almost the same."

141

A heavy silence falls as Robinson thinks about what has just been said, as he links the events of the past and Chloe's death. He doesn't want to believe it. The man is torturing him, spinning a story. Chloe's death was an accident and that wasn't in Samza's control.

"You're mad. It was an accident," says Robinson, telling himself what he wants to hear.

"It wasn't. It was a hit. Ha, see what I did there?" laughs Samza ,"a hit. Ha! And that's not the really juicy bit."

"What do you mean you piece of shit?"

"The 'hit' was paid for by your wife."

He sees the look of sheer disbelief on Robinson's face and his smile broadens. "Oh yes. The money was paid by her. £5,000."

"That money was for the tests and the data and to keep you quiet."

"Oh no it wasn't. They cost peanuts. The money paid for the hit."

Robinson staggers back, putting distance between himself and the words he doesn't want to hear.

"No."

This time Samza advances, the knife still in his hand. He wants to see Robinson's final reaction, wants to see the truth hit home.

"Her money paid for it. I organised it. I knew it would happen. How do you think I was on scene so quickly? Did you think I just heard the noise and ran out?"

"But why? Why would she do that?"

Samza's head tilted to one side as he watches closely:

"Because Chloe was going to... she was going to tell you who her father was. And Joanne couldn't face it."

Robinson shakes his head, repeatedly, from side to side. "No, no it's not true. Why would that help? Joanne would never have wanted to harm Chloe. No, it's not true."

Samza is enjoying this. He waves the knife as he makes his points, moving it to point to the left then the right:

"Let's see now. We know someone paid to have her killed, don't we? And we know it cost exactly the same money as your wife handed to me. So what? Do you think she didn't pay for Chloe to be killed? She would hardly pay for her to be just knocked over, would she?"

"What kind of a sick, twisted bastard are you? Joanne would never do that. And Chloe was killed in an accident. That's what the coroner ruled. That's what the police told me."

"But they weren't there, were they? They weren't there to hear Chloe's last words, her last, desperate plea, before she had that last little bump on her head?"

Robinson's chest tightens. A shot of adrenaline fires through his veins. His heart rate rises sharply. His voice is tight.

"What do you mean?"

Samza smiles as he hears the anger in the voice.

"Don't take on. It is all in the past now and there's nothing I can do to bring her back, is there?"

Robinson doesn't want to take the bait but he cannot help but ask.

"What do you mean by 'they weren't there?"

142

Samza knows it won't be long until Robinson will be oblivious to the pain. He has a plan. Just one more turn of the screw. Then all that's needed is for Robinson to rush forward and a hard slash across his belly will be enough. He'll exsanguinate pretty quickly and no ambulance will get here in time. Especially if there's an unavoidable delay between the severing of his intestines and the phone call. And with a friendly police force, the fact Robinson forced his way in and was trying to kill him will provide Samza with a perfect defence. He won't even be arrested let alone charged.

One more turn of the screw first though, he decides.

Robinson's voice is ice-cold as he repeats the question: "I said, what do you mean, by 'they weren't there'?"

"The police weren't there to hear her last word.

"Which was?"

"Why? She just asked why."

Robinson cannot understand this. "Why?" he repeats.

"Yes, she wanted to know why."

"Why she had been knocked down?"

Samza frowned mockingly, as if he couldn't understand how Robinson could be so wrong.

"Oh no. Not that at all."

He tightened his grip on the knife, lowering his hand, preparing for the upward thrust. Now it was time to light the fuse.

"She thanked me, you know. She thanked me for being there to help her." Samza's eyebrows rise, imitating concern: "She was in pain of course and wanted me to take the pain away. And you know, I said I would."

"That doesn't make sense. Why would she ask you why you would do that?"

"Because I said goodbye. She wanted to know why I had just said goodbye, when my hands were holding the side of her face, keeping her head up off the asphalt."

143

Samza feels the rush of raw power as he decides to administer the killer blow. One more question, one more answer and it'll be enough. He can see Robinson struggling. Not struggling to find an answer but fighting to find a way to stop the terrible but inevitable truth.

"Enough of your stupid fucking games now," he says, "Why did you say goodbye?"

Robinson's body is tense, his breathing laboured.

Samza's smile vanishes and his face takes on a stony, contemptuous look.

""You say goodbye when people leave you, She was leaving this earth then. I just helped and there was no point saying goodbye once I'd killed her, was there?"

Robinson's face shows the confusion he feels.

"You did what? But why? She was just an innocent."

"Because, Matthew Robinson, because you had to feel the pain I had felt. You had to feel the suffering of losing someone you love. It's only fair that she should have died at my hands, taken away just as you took away the one I loved."

Samza is watching closely. Robinson doesn't attack. He backs off, shaking his head in disbelief:

"So that's what this is all about? Revenge? Settling a score from an accident years ago? You're mad. And stupid," he says, "But you knew she wasn't even my daughter."

"But that's the whole point. Emma wasn't my daughter, but I loved her. And you loved Chloe. Bright, happy, blonde, vivacious, loving, curious, Chloe."

Samza gets the response he wants but he's not ready. Without warning, Robinson charges forward, yelling "YOU CUNT!" coming at him fast, too fast to step back to the counter and draw the knife back before the full force of Robinson's 240 pound body hits him, sending him flying backwards across the kitchen. His arms and legs flail outwards as he crashes to the floor, smashing his body against the stone-tiled floor a split second before his head flies backwards and then all movement stops.

Momentum carries Robinson forward, bouncing him against the countertop behind the body, making a frantic search for grip futile and he falls heavily to the floor.

He pulls himself up, ignoring the pain in his hand, his eyes focussed on Samza's still body. It's clear the man is dead. Blood is pooling beneath his head. His eyes are closed and there is no sign of breathing.

Robinson is terrified. He's not going to be able to talk his way out of this. And he's left evidence everywhere; blood on the walls, the counter, the floor and saliva too. Blood from Samza will be on his clothes too.

There is no way to claim he hasn't been here.

And there's no way to explain what happened.

Unless he finds one.

144

Robinson wants to call 999 but he knows that will put him behind bars for a long time. And he can't have that. He knows he needs to think about this.

Taking a deep breath, he stands up and begins to look through the cupboards in the kitchen. He's not sure what he's looking for but there must be something in here. Dried pulses, cereals, fruit, tins... nothing of use.

The fridge is empty, save for milk, juice and a block of butter. Next is the freezer. All that contains is a bottle of vodka. Robinson unscrews the top and takes a long slug, shuddering as the burning liquid slides down his throat, feeling the infusion of alcohol doing its work. Slamming the door shut and putting the bottle on the side, he pulls out a chair and sits down at the kitchen table, his eyes scanning the kitchen countertop.

Then they stop scanning and return to a single item. A bag of potatoes.

That'll do.

First though, he needs to deal with his hand. He rummages through the drawers to find a box of plasters, wrapping several over his finger, hoping to stem the bleeding, at least until he is ready and can leave.

Now he needs a cookbook. Or an electronic tablet. He walks through to the lounge and there it is. On the coffee table.

He picks it up, breathes a sigh of relief when he finds there is no passcode set up, and begins to google:

'Making chips.'

A click, and a list appears.

He smiles.

He clicks through several recipes and then settles on one. Taking the tablet into the kitchen, he opens the cupboard beneath the cooker and takes out a large saucepan, placing it on the stove and filling it with vegetable oil, He puts potatoes in the pan and turns the gas on to full heat. Now he's ready.

He's tempted to leave now but he has to see it start. Soon the oil begins to smoke, blue threads of smoke rising, filling the kitchen with the cloying stink of overheating oil. Any minute now, he tells himself.

The sound of a smoke detector beeping into life makes him jump, his heart pounding as he waits for the flame.

Then he remembers his fingertip. It's one bone too many.

Frantically he searches the kitchen floor for it. No sign of the end of his finger. He drops to his knees and searches under the table and around the edges of the kitchen. His head is facing away from the cooker when he hears the WHUMP as the oil catches fire.

Fuck. He can't find it. And if he doesn't find it a forensic team will know someone else was there. The flames are rising up the wall now, licking the polystyrene cornices. He watches as they catch fire and begin to melt. The acrid fumes of burning oil and plastic are catching in his throat now and he's beginning to feel nauseous. And he knows that burning polystyrene emits cyanide. There's no time. He has to get out. Unthinkingly he leans on Samza's inert body to push himself up, stopping as he is halfway up, the realisation dawning, That's it. It's got to be under the body. Desperately, Robinson pushes the body, trying to lift the sides, feeling underneath the arms and neck. He can barely see as the stinging smoke make his eyes fill with water.

He knows he can't stay any longer.

If he does, the fumes are going to kill him.

145

Yet he still doesn't leave.

His eyes are streaming and his lungs are struggling to find oxygen. Through half-open eyes he desperately makes a last-ditch attempt and hauls the body over but cannot see his fingertip on the floor. He can barely see the floor and he knows now he has got to stop looking. He's got to get out. And hope no-one finds the finger after the fire is extinguished.

He heads for the back door. About to haul it open, he remembers something about oxygen. A sudden rush of air might cause a big surge in flames. He's seen it films. Backdraft? Flashover? Either way, he leaves the back door and crawls out of the kitchen, pulling the door shut behind him. He lifts himself to his feet and hurries out of the front door, squeezing through a narrow opening before shutting it firmly behind him.

He takes a deep gasp of air and looks to both sides. No sign of anyone in the vicinity. Crossing the lawn, he reaches the street and looks back. Reassuringly there is no obvious sign of fire yet. He makes it home and slips in the back door, closing it softly and leaning back in the darkened room as he tries to slow his breathing and calm his body. Standing still, he can feel the adrenalin still coursing through him. He turns to lock the door but his hands are shaking so much, he can't even turn the key.

"Just be calm," he tells himself, a split-second before the kitchen lights burst into life. Jumping sharply, he turns to see her standing in the doorway.

"What are you doing?" he snaps.

"I might ask you exactly the same question," says Joanne. "And what have you done to your hand?"

Robinson doesn't know what to say, cannot think of an explanation.

"I, look, I didn't mean...it...."

"Sit down over here. Let me sort out your hand first. Then we talk."

146

Joanne is beginning to get frustrated. She is trying to get the details of what has happened but her husband is exhausted.

"There's no rush. Let's fix the finger and get some sleep."

"I don't want fucking sleep! I want you to tell me all of it."

"Look, it was an accident. The only way to clean up properly was a fire and I had to make it look like he left a chip pan on. Which, in a way, he did. So we have nothing to worry about and all you need to know is that there was a fire. That way, if you are questioned, you can then truthfully say you don't know. And that helps to protect me too."

"Okay, I get that. But how did you lose the bit of finger? And where is it?"

Robinson doesn't answer immediately. He thinks for a few moments, his eyes fixed on his own hand and the way her hands are wrapping his finger in a sterile bandage. He waits till she finishes and then looks up at her.

"Look Joanne, I think we need a holiday. A nice holiday somewhere far away where we can forget all about this and get some rest."

"God knows I need that, but will you just answer the question?"

"How about the Caribbean? We should be able to get a cheap enough deal, even at this time of year. We don't have to stay anywhere expensive. So long as it's clean and near a beach, that should be enough, eh?"

Joanne scowls. The thought of a holiday is tempting but she knows it will only be a temporary respite from the real world.

"I won't be able to get time off work and we haven't even started to think about it. How can we afford it? What will people think of us if we go gallivanting off on holiday only weeks after our daughters dies? I mean, what is wrong with you?"

"You need to get away from reminders. Anyone, in fact, everyone will understand that."

Robinson's reply is cut short by the sound of sirens getting closer.

Joanne hurries to the front room window to look out over at Samza's house. In front there are now three fire engines, fire officers running hoses like thick snakes across to the front of the house. Seconds later a connection is made and long plumes of spray shoot up into the air and towards the flaming torch that was once a home. Clouds of steam, sparks and ash fly high up into the sky, dissipating into the night and floating down towards the ground in a wide radius. An ambulance appears and parks up farther away, waiting, presumably, for anyone still alive to be got out.

Which seems unlikely. The flames have really got hold and the entire roof is burning, the heat and the risk of collapse pushing the firefighters back from the building.

Robinson has followed her and is staring out with her. He stands beside her, arms folded, the reflection of flickering lights broken by the intensity of the fire.

"Christ, that looks bad, doesn't it?" he says cheerily.

She looks round and sees his face, his eyes open wide as he takes in the scale of the fire. She sees surprise, awe and something else. Satisfaction? His eyes catch hers and she knows. Not the details but she knows.

"Maybe a holiday *is* a good idea," she says, "let's book."

147

Neither of them sleeps well. Blaming it on the unfamiliar bed, the overheated hotel and the air-conditioning are just excuses. They know what's disturbing them. It's not discussed openly. It lurks beside them, an unpleasant bulk in the atmosphere, a block to every conversation.

"Come on, he says, let's just go, shall we?"

They leave the hotel and walk across the concourse to the check in zones. Robinson had persuaded Joanne that it would be better to check in on the day of travel; a means of giving no warning and preventing anything stopping them getting away. Getting away on holiday, he had added guiltily.

So they walk towards the check in desks, handing over passports and paperwork. waiting for the usual questions. But the girl behind the counter seems distracted. She keeps looking at a piece of paper that has been taped to her computer screen. Robinson can feel his heart rate going up as he watches, trying to appear nonchalant and disinterested. The pulse at his neck tells a different story.

Joanne looks terrified. She keeps swallowing.

"Is everything alright?" she asks the girl.

"Oh yes. It's all fine. I just have to do a few operational checks that's all. If you can just be a little patient, we'll have this sorted out very quickly."

Joanne takes a deep breath and turns to Robinson, putting her hand on his arm, telling him she can't wait to be lying on a hot sunny beach with a margarita in hand, trying to conjure up a picture that will calm them both.

"Me too," says Robinson, his back to the counter as he scans the airport around him. It's busy but not packed full of people and he can see most travellers heading towards the check in desks with luggage trolleys. Here and there he can see people with cases checking watches, looking at boards, waiting for someone to arrive. His gaze drifts along the rows of airline counters and sees a couple of men standing together. No bags. Not looking at notice boards. Just waiting. And trying not to look as though they are scanning the desks.

He swallows and takes a deep breath. No cause for panic, he tells himself. His gaze moves on, past the counters and over to the opposite end of the row of desks. And his eyes widen as an armed policeman nudges his colleague and the two of them begin to walk purposefully towards him. He can see they are still some distance away. Fear bubbles up inside him and he looks for an escape. The exit to the car park is barely twenty metres away. If he runs now, he'll make it before they catch him. And they are not likely to shoot an unarmed man, are they?

But there's no point. He won't make it to a car and there's nowhere he can feasibly disappear from sight. Not in an airport. He's about to say something to Jo when he hears the words he is dreading:

"Mr and Mrs Robinson?" asks the girl, looking at her counter screen and avoiding eye contact.

"I am afraid there's a bit of a problem."

148

Robinson looks at the girl and then at Joanne, trying to read an answer in her eyes. He looks once more at the armed policeman and his shoulders drop. There's no time to make it to the carpark now. All he can do is wait.

The girl behind the counter starts to speak.

"I'm sorry but we have had to change your seats. We've upgraded you to business class. Two seats together in the middle of the row, if that's okay?"

Joanne replies they are both happy with that, reaching out to touch Robinson's arm, subconsciously drawing him into the conversation. Robinson forces himself to look away from the police and pay attention to the counter. By the time he turns around, the officers have left the check-in area.

Once the boarding passes have been handed over, they listen to the instructions on how to find the airline lounge and thank the airline representative for the upgrade, before making their way upstairs and into the hushed lounge area. They take seats in comfortable armchairs, the view of the runway to one side, and Robinson holds his hand out, palm upward, waiting for her hand to reach his.

"We'll be fine," he tells her, smiling broadly. "Let's forget about everything for now, shall we. Just enjoy ourselves. After all, we are on our way to sunshine, beaches and cocktails. And ten days of peace and relaxation."

Then he sees the bar area.

"Champagne?"

Jo nods, takes her hand back and pulls out a book from her bag. "Get a snack or two, will you?" she says quietly.

Robinson nods and heads over to the bar. There are two men in front of him as he gets there, both pouring out fruit juice. He steps back when they finish and glances at them as they pass him, giving a half-smile to avoid being rude. A smile that clears immediately when he realises they are the two men from the check-in area. He turns to watch them taking seats near the exit to the lounge, the better to watch their targets.

'Get a grip,' he tells himself. 'You're being stupid. They are probably just two ordinary people on a work trip somewhere. He takes a breath, pours a couple of glasses of champagne and heads back to Joanne.

The moment he reaches her he realises he has forgotten the snacks. After another journey to the drinks bar, he returns, puts a bowl of crisps on the table between them and opens up a newspaper. He scans for any mention of the death when she interrupts him.

"Matthew," she says, her tone indicating a real problem. "Look at this."

She shows him a posting on her social media feed. There is a photograph of the ruins of the doctor's house with a comment: 'Looks like the doctor torched his own house!' #Arson#Missing

She starts to scroll through the entries and learns that the house was completely gutted. That there is no sign of Dr Samza, except for a piece of finger. The police are working on the theory that Samza was tortured and then kidnapped, the house being torched either as revenge or to cover up evidence.

Robinson is silent. Even though he is sitting in an airport lounge before flying off on holiday, he's not sure he'll be able to truly enjoy the holiday. And he can't do anything about the thing that's bothering him. Not till they are back anyway.

Then he can find out what happened to Samza's body.

Printed in Great Britain
by Amazon